Journey in the Waiting is the c[...]
specifically for the middle sch[...]
schoolers, the amazing Biblical l[...]
many Bible based concepts along[...]
reader of all ages. This last work of fiction in the trilogy is an excellent example of the scripture that says, "Trust in the Lord with all your heart, and lean not on your own understanding; In all your ways acknowledge Him, and He shall direct your paths." (Prov. 3:5.) It's a story of loss, prayer and trusting God, while waiting for His answer. Although our ways are not God's ways, (His ways are so much higher than ours! Isa. 55:8,9) His answer will indeed come...all in His timing!! *Journey in the Waiting* will encourage the reader that no matter what trial they may face; God's love for them is great and He will make a way. In our current culture, *Journey in the Waiting* is a breath of fresh air... I know every child will enjoy this adventure...and be completely encouraged along the way!!

    Kathy Lesnoff, President/CEO Mosaic Pregnancy & Health Centers

I loved *Journey in the Waiting* because it shows the benefits of trusting God. Tea and Johann have to trust that God will help them find their lost daughter and Meta. The faith that this couple has is beyond imagining. *Journey in the Waiting* shows how trust in God grows stronger through every struggle. This book piqued my interest because it shows that with faith in God, anything is possible.

    Natalia, age 13

The Journey books are really great! Kids and adults will enjoy reading all three books because there are characters who are young and old. The story is also very interesting and a little mysterious with a few bad guys, but one really good guy, God, who makes everything better. I wasn't sure how the whole story would end, but I like how D Marie wrote each book so I wanted to keep reading more. The pictures are really good, too. I think everyone should take time to read not just one of the books, but the whole trilogy!

    Joby Nelson, age 10 and author of *The Underdog Gang* book series

Journey in the Waiting is the last book of a three-part book series. There are many Bible references scattered frequently throughout the book with a lesson in each. This is a story of loss, but also hope, because with God, all things are possible. This book shows to you that sometimes it may not seem like God is on your side, like if you have lost a loved one. But despite whatever you say or do, God will always be on your side. Which is something that a lot of people need to know. *Journey in the Waiting* will let every kid and adult know that no matter what obstacles or trials you face, God is on your side. Everyone who reads this book will be enlightened with the truth, and this will make their day.

    Jacob Staake, age 12

Journey in the Waiting

Journey in the Waiting

D Marie

Illustrated by

Reverend Brian King

Copyright © 2021 by D Marie

All rights reserved. No part of this book may be used or reproduced by any means, graphic, electronic, or mechanical, including photocopying, recording, taping or by any information storage retrieval system without the written permission of the author except in the case of brief quotations embodied in critical articles and reviews.

Scripture taken from the King James Version of the Bible

This is the work of fiction. All of the characters, names, incidents, organizations, and dialogue in this novel are either the products of the author's imagination or are used fictitiously.

WWW.DMarieBooks.com

Certain stock imagery © Shutterstock
Certain stock imagery © Getty Images

ISBN: 978-1-7340520-6-0

Library of Congress Control Number: 2021902159

Printed in the United States of America

Dedication

*My Children, Craig and Dee Ann,
who dedicate their lives to share the
Word of God and serve His people*

Special Acknowledgement

The Lord, my Healer, for the inspiration for this book

Contents

Introduction

1 The Plan 1

2 Promotion 7

3 Searching 15

4 Geir 23

5 Compassion 33

6 New Beginnings 41

7 Father and Son 53

8 Meta and Anna at Sea 65

9 Artz 69

10 Live Life One Day at a Time 75

11 Taulbe Castle 81

12 Following the Trail 87

13 River Work 97

14 The Long Summer 103

15 Ari's Agony 109

16 Home 117

17 Hopelessness to Hope 123

18 New Student 131

19 Good News, Bad News 137

20 Letters 145

21 Winter 155

22 Winter Ends 163

23 Spring 171

24 Summer 185

25 Fall 189

Discussion Starters 195

Reflections 198

Acknowledgements 199

About the Author and Artists 201

Book Description 203

Introduction

Journey in the Waiting completes the trilogy of faith, family, and forgiveness. *Journey to the Glass Hill* and *Journey to the Noble Horse* are the first two books.

The Glass Hill story demonstrates how bitterness has adverse effects on a person's life and the lives of those closest to them. When the person repents of such bitterness, the Lord provides His forgiveness and helps the person to turn their life around.

The Noble Horse story demonstrates how jealousy leads to resentment and the desire to punish others. This is also a redeemable condition for the repentant person. The Lord is waiting to fight for anyone who steps out in faith. His answer may not be what they have planned, but His ways are higher than our ways.

This story, *Journey in the Waiting*, is about healing. There are many hurts that people endure as they journey through life. Sometimes, while they are going through their trials and tribulations, their answer to prayer comes when they focus on others instead of their immediate need.

Wherever your journey in life takes you, keep your eyes focused on the Lord and He will make your paths straight (Proverbs 3:6).

Enjoy the Journey,
D Marie

Chapter 1

The Plan

The noon sun shone brightly. White, fluffy clouds dotted the blue sky. Green trees gently swayed in the light breeze. The aroma of flowers drifted from the neighboring garden. But neither the sun, the breeze, nor the gentle fragrance of flowers could wash away the stench of defeat.

Silence prevailed except for the neighing of the nearby horses. The horde of captured men huddled together, afraid to make a sound. The palace guards would be merciful but only to a point. These marauders had just attacked their palace and had wounded some of their fellow comrades-in-arms. With swords drawn, emotions ran high.

The weight of the destruction and blood shed bore down on King Albert's shoulders. After all, this was his palace and he had failed to protect his family, friends, and perhaps the whole kingdom. If the Edelross horse hadn't trampled the Hawk Man, the outcome would had been entirely and devastatingly different. Sunrays reflected off Albert's blondish hair, revealing a few strands of gray. He tightened his square jaw, quietly assessing everyone's needs and what the next course of action should be. His squeezed fists turned white in an attempt to defuse his emotions. Grateful that no one in his family or friends had suffered an injury, Albert let a sigh of relief escape his lips.

Not all were relieved. He watched his father-by-marriage, King Stefan of Herrgott, grieve. Mournful groans flowed from Stefan while he walked next to the litter carrying the lifeless body of his son. Stefan had journeyed to Christana to witness his great-granddaughter's baptism. His son, Stefan the Younger, known as Falke the Hawk Man, had interrupted the ceremony with an orchestrated attack. Consumed with jealousy, the Hawk Man had wanted to destroy everyone who had hindered his happiness, but revenge doesn't produce contentment.

In his final moments, Stefan the Younger found the love and peace that had eluded his soul when he gave his life to Jesus. But now Albert needed to decide what to do with the men Stefan the Younger had deceived into following his devious plan.

Watching his wife, Queen Maria, comfort their daughter, Princess Tea, pain gripped Albert's heart. Just a few moments ago, Stefan the Younger had pointed his sword at Tea, demanding to know where Tea's baby daughter, Anna, was hidden.

Stefan the Younger had been sitting on the white Edelross stallion when he had pointed his sword at Tea. The enraged man's father, King Stefan, had intervened by walking toward the horse with his arms in the air. Responding to the visual cue, the horse had reared straight up on his hind legs. Caught off guard, Stefan the Younger had dropped his sword and tumbled to the ground. Unfortunately, the horse's hoofs had come down on top of the rider's chest and mortally wounded him.

His death had prompted his men to throw down their armaments and surrender. Their lives now rested in the hands of the ruler of Christana, King Albert.

The Head Guard gave a preliminary report. "Sire, the attackers claim they were sent here by your request to protect you and your family from a rebellion. They believed the lies from this man they call Falke and followed his orders."

King Albert stared at the horse gate, watching his father-by-marriage return. The elderly king's ashen face gave no indication of immediate advice. Albert drew in a deep breath and slowly released it. "Lord, I need wisdom," he whispered.

Journey in the Waiting

"What shall I do? Please allow someone to be Your voice to help us."

Tea pushed back strands of her blond tresses and surveyed the field of prisoners. Her joyful spirit was crushed. She looked at her husband, Johann, with her woeful grayish-blue eyes. "I need some solitude to pray for our baby. Meta escaped with her, but where did they go? Will she be alright? Anna will be hungry soon."

Johann gathered Tea in his embrace while her arms hung limp by her side. "Tea, I'll go with you."

"No!" Tea pushed back. "Go get our daughter and bring her home. Mama and I will go and pray."

Strands of Maria's normally coiffed brown hair hung by the sides of her face in ringlets. Connecting her eyes with Tea's, she reached for her daughter's hand and led her away to a quiet place to reflect on the day's events and comfort her daughter. What started as a day of joy with her granddaughter's baptism had ended in her brother's death. While walking away on the path to the garden, Maria offered a prayer and forgave her brother and the invading guards. Suddenly, she stopped. Dropping her daughter's hand, she spun around and walked back toward her husband.

Squinting her grayish eyes, Maria surveyed the grassy field. With her hands on her hips, she yelled for all to hear, "These men did evil. They weren't born this way. They were deceived and believed a lie. If they're willing, let them repent. Let them learn of the Lord's love but pay the consequences of their behavior. Search each one of them thoroughly to make sure they do not possess any more weapons.

"They need an opportunity to be constructive. This town could use some work. Walls need to be repaired. Roads need to be paved. Father, are there any projects you wish to be accomplished? These men should be integrated back into a productive life. Give them reading and writing lessons if needed. Most importantly, watch their behavior. As for the guard who whispered in my brother's ear and wanted to hurt my daughter, he needs to have a severe consequence. He cannot be trusted until he proves himself trustworthy again."

The men's jaws dropped, including Tea's.

"Uh...uh..." Albert uttered. He swallowed. "Thank You, Lord. This is perfect!" Inquisitive eyes turned to Albert. "I had just prayed for the Lord to allow someone to be His voice. This is a Spirit-filled directive."

A clanging noise in the foreground caught their attention. Concealed knives were being tossed to the ground near the palace guards. Not all of the captured men understood the Christanan language, but they grasped the intent and mimicked the actions of the ones who did understand. All but one of the attacking guards had worried looks on their faces. The one holdout was the guard Maria had mentioned, the one who had whispered in her brother's ear. Drawing his eyelids into narrow slits, Lochen crossed his arms and glared at his captors.

As the men pondered on Maria's words, Benjamin came out of the palace with his son, Josef. Tea walked over and picked up the young boy. Josef blinked his brown eyes in amazement. Tea had never held him before.

"I will care for Josef here at the palace just as if he were my own son, Benjamin," Tea said looking reassuringly in Benjamin's eyes. "My uncle's last words were 'Anna is safe.' I believe those words. It means your wife is safe, too. Meta and Anna will return home."

"Thank you, Princess Tea," Benjamin began. "Knowing Josef is taken care of lets me concentrate on the journey ahead. We need to leave right away."

Johann patted Benjamin on the back. "I'll be right back." Then he ran inside the palace.

Gunther, the horse handler, nodded and left to get the horses for the men going on the journey. One of the guards left to gather provisions necessary for the ride: food and bedrolls, if needed, for the men and milk for the baby.

One of the ministers, Ivar, took the hands of his betrothed. "Petra, we'll hurry as fast as we can."

"Ivar," Petra began, "I'm relieved that you and Magnus are going. Johann needs both of his brothers for support."

"Pray for us. I have a queasy feeling in my gut. I'm hoping it's just from all of the turmoil we went through today."

"I will. The Lord will provide and heal us from this tragedy."

Ivar embraced Petra one more time and mounted his horse.

Magnus, the other minister, said his goodbyes to Petra's cousin, "Angela, I'm thankful you're here for Petra. With all of my family gone, she would have been alone at the farm."

Angela had arrived in Christana with King Stefan just two weeks ago. Her real purpose for coming was to meet the minister her cousin had written about in her letter, Magnus. Angela let out a little sigh and replied, "Petra and I will pray for your safe return." She added, "May the Lord guide you all safely to baby Anna and Meta."

Magnus gave an assuring smile. "When I return, I would like to send a letter to your parents." Angela beamed. She knew what that meant.

As he reached for her hand, his father, Ari, yelled, "Mount up, everyone. It's time to go."

Pursing his lips, Magnus waved goodbye.

Johann, not wanting to draw any attention to his position being a prince, returned dressed in common clothes. Standing by his wife and Josef, he draped an arm around Tea's shoulders and wiped her tears with his free hand. Turning his head toward his horse, Johann gritted his teeth, trying to ward off any tears that wanted to flow.

Pushing the chestnut brown hair to the side, Benjamin kissed his son's face. "Josef, you will stay here at the palace with Tea." The boy turned his head sideways and gave his father an odd look. Benjamin whispered in his son's ear, "Tea needs someone to play with. Could you do that for me?"

D Marie

"Yes, Papa," Josef replied. "I know some games we can play."

Benjamin looked up at Tea. "Thank you," he silently mouthed before quickly mounting his horse.

Tea opened her mouth but choked up. A new tear dripped down her cheek.

Albert remained at the palace to deal with the attacking guards. King Stefan stayed behind to bury his only son.

"Ari," Albert said, "I'll personally see that your farm is taken care of."

"Thank you. Benjamin's brother, Klaus, is still there. He'll appreciate the help."

The palace guards opened the horse gate, and the five men started the journey to bring Meta and Anna back home.

Chapter 2

Promotion

Albert stretched out his hand and laid it on Stefan's shoulder. The elderly man's chest heaved in and out. Stefan momentarily squeezed his eyes closed, contemplating his next move. Tears ran down his face and dropped onto his jacket. Albert and Stefan exchanged a few words before they headed toward the courtyard garden. They both nodded. Taking a deep breath, Stefan looked at the horse caretaker. "Gunther, come with us."

Gunther unconsciously rubbed his beard, dragging his thumb across his facial scar. *Perhaps, they want me to help with the horses the attacking guards rode*, he surmised. *We don't have enough stalls.*

Albert picked a secluded area with benches near the fountain. He hoped the sound of the bubbling water would soothe their troubled souls. He waited for everyone to sit down. "Gunther, we're going to need your help."

"I'm at your service, King Albert."

"Gunther, we have known each other for a long time. We grew up together when I lived in Herrgott many years ago. You have always shown your loyalty to me and Stefan. You never told anyone about Falke's relationship to my family. Gunther, I wish I would have done this sooner. I want you to be part of our family. Please call me by my given name at all times."

Gunther leaned backward. His dark brown eyes opened wide to access this invitation. *To call the king by his name at all times is a position higher than Ari's, and Ari's son is Albert's son-by-marriage. His granddaughter is Princess*

Anna. After Gunther thought about it, he replied, "I am not worthy of this honor, King Albert."

"All the more reason for choosing you, Gunther. Now, try it. Call me Albert."

Gunther lowered his head. "Albert."

"Yes, Gunther?" Albert replied. "Well done. Now, we have serious business to discuss."

"Do you wish for me to get something?"

"No, we want your input regarding Maria's plan. This is not an easy task."

"I suggest," Gunther began causing the two men to lean toward him. "I suggest we send a detachment of guards to Falke Castle. There may be more men there that do not know the true situation. When we get there, we would need to convince them of the truth and then offer them a chance to surrender. But do we give them the same consequences as those that attacked us here at the palace?"

"Good thinking," Stefan added. The silver headed man reached for his beard. Finding only smooth skin, he puckered his mouth. He had removed it prior to the journey to Christana to disguise his appearance. "We need to send couriers to Herrgott and inform my guards of the situation as soon as possible."

"Gunther," Albert remarked, "your insight is helpful. You're thinking like a person in charge. Would you like to select a group of our guards and lead them to the castle? All of the guards there should be put under arrest until we can be assured that their future behavior will not put any citizen at risk."

"Yes, it would be my honor." Gunther bowed to the two kings, letting his dark brown hair flow forward. Immediately, he straightened up. "Albert." Gunther paused as he used this unfamiliar form of addressing the king. "I have looked at Falke's men. Most of them are still under the age of twenty. Some of them don't have very much facial hair. They look like children."

"All the more reason to retrain them," Albert said. "They can still be saved, mentally and spiritually. The Lord can heal these men and these boys."

"King Stefan," Gunter started, but Stefan threw his hand up.

"Gunther, please call me by my name in all circumstances."

Gunther looked at Albert who smiled and nodded. Gunther had grown up on King Stefan's palace grounds. This would be another honor and a more difficult habit to break.

"Stefan," Gunther began with a slight hesitation in his voice, "can we keep the guards at my Uncle Gustav's ferry?"

"Of course, before we change our procedures, we'll keep all of our protective measures in place."

"Stefan," Gunther continued with a little more ease this time, "when we take over Falke Castle, it will propose another challenge."

"What is the challenge?" Stefan asked intently, causing his eyebrows to draw together.

"The castle is difficult to quickly access from Herrgott and keep it monitored. Would it be possible to build a bridge over the Vogel River next to Falke Castle?"

Stefan slammed his fist on his bench. "No!"

Gunther turned pale. *Maybe I overstepped my new freedom,* Gunther thought and quickly replied, "My apologies, Sire."

"Gunther, I wasn't talking about the bridge. I mean the castle name. Falke was a name of rebellion used by my son. It's time to get rid of that defiant title. Do you have any suggestions?"

Gunther's mouth went dry. *I'm given a chance to rename the castle.* He looked around the palace garden. He closed his eyes and thought of the hawk image on the attackers' tunics. Looking at the two kings, he revealed his thoughts, "Everyone knows that I like horses." The two kings' eyes brightened.

"I also like birds. The hawk is a predator and was used as a symbol of evil. I suggest a symbol of goodness: Taulbe."

"Dove!" Albert exclaimed. "It's a symbol of the Holy Spirit. What are your thoughts, Stefan?"

"This is an excellent choice, Taulbe Castle will be a beacon of peace and protection for the those who travel by the converging rivers. Now, let's talk about that bridge. I'll have my counselors look into the construction. This sounds like a good project for our future construction workers sitting in the horse pasture."

"Those workers will need to be fed and have a place to sleep," Albert added. "The mares' stable is big enough. There's only one way in and out. We'll put the mares and their foals in the corral." Deep furrows grew in the space between Albert's eyebrows. His eyelids narrowed to a thin line. "As for that defiant man, Lochen, he needs to be separated from the group and secured in the dungeon. He could cause insurrection or disorder with the other guards."

"May I offer another suggestion?" Gunther asked.

"Please do," Albert replied.

"Have all of the attacking guards discard anything with the hawk symbol on it—including tunics."

"Excellent," Stefan commended. "I suggest we reduce the number of prisoners that are confined together. It lessens their chances of overpowering our palace guards."

"A wise idea," Albert agreed. "The young men need to be in a group away from the older ones. We have some tents. It would be a temporary solution until better housing is devised."

"Will Taulbe Castle be a suitable place of retention until the attackers are reformed and trained?" Gunther asked.

"That castle is better suited than this palace or mine," Stefan added. "We need to fortify Taulbe Castle with plenty of guards. I have a surplus, and they speak the same language as the attackers."

"Wise idea," Albert said. "The sooner we can transport them, the better. I don't want them here as a reminder of today's events. My family has endured too much."

Journey in the Waiting

"Would you like to stay at the castle and oversee the requirements for this transition and maintenance of the attackers?" Stefan asked Gunther.

"Yes, I would! You can depend on me."

"Gunther," Albert began, "could you be ready to leave tomorrow by first light to subdue the current garrison and fortify the castle with our guards?"

"Yes, I will select a group of guards immediately. Perhaps, I should go help with the sleeping arrangements and the discarding of the tunics."

"Good, I never want to see that hawk symbol again." Albert's clinched fists turned his knuckles white.

"I want one," Stefan softly added, staring at the ground. "I want a reminder. Allowing malevolent behavior to grow can lead to disaster."

Gunther stood up and laid his hand on Stefan's shoulder. Stefan placed his hand on top of Gunther's. Unspoken words conveyed their feelings. Gunther quietly walked away. After a few moments, Albert and Stefan followed.

Entering the horse pasture, Gunther noticed the palace guards already busily stacking discarded hawk tunics. "The men didn't want to be associated with the Hawk Man anymore," a guard told Gunther. "They wanted to be free of that life."

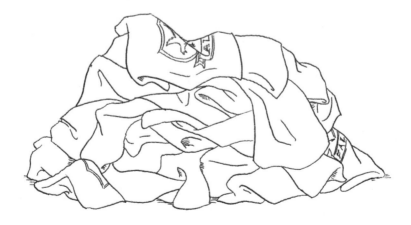

Frowning, Gunther looked around the horse pasture and saw Lochen sitting by himself, still wearing his tunic and squinting his black, beady eyes at the rest of the captives. His hands had been tied behind his back.

"This one was causing trouble with the other men," the same palace guard said, pointing to Lochen. "We didn't ask anyone to discard their tunics. He became angry when the group voluntarily took them off. Then he became aggressive and started to hit the others. We had to subdue him. The prisoners held him down while we tied his hands behind his back."

Gunther was amazed but not surprised. *Albert,* he thought, *you were right about this man.* "Guard, you did well to separate and confine that man. He's to be transferred to the dungeon immediately by the order of King Albert."

Lochen heard Gunther's words. His lips curled into a smug smirk. Deep hatred emanated from his eyes. His irises looked like they were burning with sulfur. When Lochen was escorted from the pasture, the other prisoners cheered. Lochen started to yell at them but was quickly gagged.

On his way to the dungeon, Lochen saw the kings of Christana and Herrgott approaching the horse gate. He gave the monarchs a look that sent cold chills down their spines. The guards noticed and turned Lochen's body in a different direction. Albert and Stefan returned to the secluded space.

"I'm responsible for all of this," Stefan confessed.

"Stefan," Albert interrupted, "you are not responsible for another person's actions."

"But I allowed my son to grow in these adverse behaviors. He was jealous of you when you lived with us. I tried to make up for his jealousies by giving him everything he wanted. I was a permissive father to him."

"You're also Maria's father, and you were a wonderful father with her," Albert noted. "Your son chose to let those negative attitudes dwell in his heart." Albert took a deep breath and continued, "I'm to blame, too."

Stunned, Stefan stared at Albert. "How can this be? You're a true man of God."

"My guilt lies with the Edelross horses. If I had never asked for them, then Stefan the Younger may have never tried to harm us. I put my family's lives in jeopardy."

"Albert, the reason I didn't give my son the special breed of horses is because he wanted to train the Edelrosses for war. You wanted them for a noble purpose. That was the first time I told him no, and he didn't like it. From that point on, he moved into rebellion. I didn't know how to stop it. Our relationship had died."

Albert embraced his father-by-marriage. "Stefan, I had no idea."

"I'm glad I finally told someone. I've been harboring this deep hurt way too long."

Albert's chest raised in a deep sigh. "We need to pray for healing. And pray for the safety of our baby and Meta and their return home."

Stefan nodded. Bowing their heads, the two kings prayed. Stefan's crusty exterior crumbled for a moment and relief flooded his heart.

While they prayed, Gunther took over command of the disposition of the prisoners. Since Lochen was no longer in sight, the other men were most compliant. The prisoners, younger than twenty, were separated from the older ones. The younger men assembled the tents for their lodging. The older men cleaned the horse stable and added fresh straw on the floor. Each prisoner graciously accepted a bedroll.

One of the prisoner's stomach growled when the food was delivered. The captured guards hadn't eaten since the night before. They meekly accepted the food and remained quiet. After the meal, one of the prisoners asked if he could speak with Gunther. The request was granted.

"Sir," the prisoner began, "common sense dictates you'll be going to Falke Castle. I can help you to get through the woods on the trail we took getting here. It'll be quicker. The guards at the castle know me. I can talk to them and persuade them to open the gate and lay down their arms. I can also show you where our campsite is. You should retrieve the rest of our belongings."

"I'll consider your request," Gunther replied. "You need to return to your group." Gunther cupped his bearded face. He watched the neatly groomed prisoner turn away, hanging his head. "Wait! What is your name?"

The captive twirled around. "Gabriel, Sir."

"It's a good name. Are you a good person, Gabriel?"

"No, Sir," he answered lowering his head. "I am a sinner. I have sinned against God and the people here."

"Gabriel, when you go back to the stable, sleep near the door. It will make it easier to find you before first light."

A smile appeared on Gabriel's face and his eyes brightened. He was a young man of twenty-five years. His contrite heart wanted to repent.

After all the prisoners laid down for the night, several guards with torches kept watch around the pasture. Gunther walked into the stable for the stallions. He patted his horses and called them by their names. When he got to the end of the stable, he drew in a deep breath and slowly released it. He had to say goodbye to his friends, the Edelross horses.

Bobbing his head, the mighty white Edelross nickered, listening to Gunther. "Be patient with Ari when he gets back. He's a good trainer and will take excellent care of you. I have taught him everything I know. I hope to see you soon, my friend."

The younger Edelrosses had finished their color changes and were now pure white, no longer the brown and black of their youth. They nodded their heads over their stable door, whinnying for their master to visit them, too. Gunther appreciated the solitude of the stable. He wouldn't want anyone to see him in this emotional state. Tears stung his eyes. "Goodbye, my friends," he said one more time before walking to the barracks for the night.

Chapter 3

Searching

Several hoofprints pointed toward Christana, but only one set traveled north. Meta's horse left a very distinctive pattern in the dirt to track. One of the horseshoes was partially broken off.

"The prints haven't been disturbed since Meta rode in this direction," said Ari. "By the depth of the tracks, she's keeping up her pace."

"Meta, we're coming. Hang on, dear," Benjamin muttered. His normally upright shoulders slumped. A shadow of apprehension hung over his walnut-colored eyes, robbing them of their normal glowing shine. When the wind blew his brown hair around, he never patted it back in place.

Johann silently prayed, *Jesus, keep my little girl safe. Make sure Meta holds her tight. It's not easy to ride with a baby in your lap.*

The twins, Magnus and Ivar, eyed each other while they continually mouthed every prayer they could think of from their seminary training. Momentarily closing his eyes, Ivar asked a silent request. *Holy Spirit, take my humble words and lay them down at the feet of Jesus. Help us find Meta and the baby so we can bring them home. Put Your arm of protection around them and keep them safe. In Your Name I pray, Jesus. Amen.*

Silence enveloped the group. Perhaps, they reflected on the danger of just a few hours ago.

D Marie

"Lord," Johann spoke out lifting his face up, "thank You for saving us. Without Your help, we would be at the mercy of Falke."

The other four riders eyed this fair-headed prince. "Amen."

A discussion followed about how the intruders had entered the palace property with little difficulty. Even though the guards were on alert, a crack in their defense existed.

Ari straightened his sturdy frame in his saddle. His sons matched him in height and size but still had much to learn. The twins favored their father's dark hair and brown eyes, but Johann had his mother's golden hair and blue eyes. Although Ari's brown curly hair was slowly changing into a subtle gray, he still had the muscular strength of his younger days. His weathering skin indicated years of working in the fields.

He pondered on the discussion, made an analogy of his life, and then compared it to what had happened at the palace. "When my Johanna died, the enemy came in and brought bitterness and anger. I carried it for years. When I finally recognized the cruel captivity I was shrouded in, I asked Jesus for help. He set me free. Now, I keep my guard up. It's not a pain free life, but it is a better life."

The three brothers looked at each other. Without saying a word, they shared the pleasant feeling that their father, who used to run away from God, now runs to Him.

It remained quiet for a few more miles before Magnus spoke. "Benjamin, you chose a great horse to follow. These tracks are easy to find. It looks like Meta slowed up after a few miles from Christana. Perhaps she felt safe from the attackers."

"I'm thankful she kept on the path while holding the baby," Benjamin noted. "She must have been watching closely when others were riding their horses. She hasn't ridden that often."

"Women are more capable than what they get acknowledged for," Johann replied. "When given an opportunity, they do excel. Maria really surprised me today. She had great wisdom to share."

"She even made the prisoners nervous," Ari noted. All the men gave a small chuckle. "Benjamin, how well does Meta know these roads?"

"We have visited her sister in Geir only a few times," Benjamin replied. "I always drove the team of horses pulling the wagon. Meta has never traveled by herself. Geir is the last village off the trail. We always enjoyed seeing the beach and sea when we arrived."

"Father," Johann asked, "have you been there before?"

"Yes," Ari replied, "we've usually sold all of our horses before we reached Geir, but your brothers and I sometimes visited the other villages to see if there was a need for trained horses."

"The reputation of our horses was very good," Magnus shared. "Many villagers would tell their friends and neighbors about them, and we would be well received by every village. We never had any problems."

"Papa," Ivar asked, "are we near the rock arrow?"

"What's the rock arrow?" Benjamin asked.

"When I first traveled north to sell my horses, I often ended up on a side path accidently. There is nothing in that direction, and the path ends after a few miles," Ari shared. "So, I created a group of stones pointing in the correct direction."

"I remember that group of rocks," Benjamin said. "That was you who put them there? Thanks. It was a landmark for me to look for."

"Ivar," Magnus asked, "do you remember our first trip with father? We were both wide-eyed with excitement."

"I remember. You wouldn't leave father's side."

Magnus frowned and his mind drifted to his other brother. "Johann, while we were gone, did you ever ride that black stallion?"

Johann made a few throat noises and mildly replied, "Yes, one time. It was a bareback ride."

"I knew it," Ari said out loud. "I'm proud of you, Son. That is one cantankerous horse. You have to be a great horseman for him to allow you to ride on his back."

"You were very dependable, Johann," Ivar added. "The farm and the animals were always well taken care of during our absence."

"When I look back on those times, I see them as good learning experiences for my future position in life," Johann said. "It always amazes me how God can take something difficult and make something beneficial out of it."

"It requires faith, dear brother," Ivar contributed. "You pioneered that behavior for all of us to follow. Thank you, Johann."

For the first time since the attack, Johann had a faint smile playing on his lips as he reflected on Ivar's words. *I have to be a rock now. I'm the sovereign in charge. The others will be looking to me to be strong.*

As evening approached, storm clouds rolled in. It was getting difficult to see, but none of the men wanted to stop following the tracks. When the rain began, the hoofprints disappeared and transformed into mud.

"We need to stop at all of the villages from now on," Ari said. "We have to see if Meta stopped at any of them."

Lighting streaked through the blackened sky, offering momentary illumination. Loud thunder quickly followed, startling the horses. "Papa!" Magnus yelled. "A building ahead; it's an inn."

Leaning forward in the saddle, everyone rushed toward the faint light. They quickly tethered their horses and went inside. Water dripped from their clothing, leaving puddles on the floor. The heat from the fireplace beckoned them to stand nearby and warm up their bodies while their clothes dried. Immediately, the innkeeper came from the backroom to address their needs.

Benjamin headed for the innkeeper. "Have you seen a woman with a baby today traveling through?"

"Yes," the innkeeper replied, "her baby was very hungry and wanted to be fed. Normally, I don't have milk, so I had to have a neighbor bring some in a milk container. She drank it very quickly."

"Did she and the baby stay here?" Johann anxiously asked.

"No," the innkeeper replied, "she said her family was expecting her and wanted to make use of the remaining daylight. She left and continued her journey." The innkeeper continued, "Would you men be interested in staying the night? A meal can be quickly prepared, and I can provide food and shelter for your horses in the adjoining stable."

They all locked eyes with the same thought to continue, but all of them decided it was wise to continue the search during the daylight tomorrow. Even though the food was good, everyone consumed only half of it. The innkeeper noticed. "I'll have a morning meal prepared for you before first light. Your horses will be fed, watered, and curried. Your rooms are ready. Good night, sirs."

The men remained quiet. They just nodded to the innkeeper and went to the sleeping rooms. Clean sheets and blankets covered the beds. The walls and windows helped to muffle the sound of the rain. Soon, all the searchers fell asleep.

Before first light, the innkeeper entered his cooking area. Pulling the food from the lauder, he carefully laid his future breakfast on his preparation table. After poking the embers in the fireplace, a flame regained its intensity and licked at the new supply of wood. Picking up a large pot of water, the innkeeper clanged his pot on the kettle hanging in the fireplace. Using a metal spoon, he made exaggerated noises striking the stirring bowl and letting the plates and utensils drop on the table. "These men need an early start. I'll wake them up."

When Ari walked to the tables, the innkeeper greeted him with open arms. "Ari, good to see you! I didn't recognize you last night."

Tilting his head, Ari scrunched his eyebrows together and just stared at him for a moment. Then he smiled, realizing he had been in this village before.

"Are the two you're looking for family?" the innkeeper asked.

"The baby is my granddaughter, and the woman is my friend's wife."

"Five men looking for a young woman and a baby?" the innkeeper inquired with a curious look on his face.

Being careful, Ari replied, "She had to quickly get to her sister's village, but the reason to leave is no longer necessary."

"Have your men enjoy their morning meal. I'll bring your horses around to the front. They are rested and saddled."

Ari nodded. After eating, everyone made their way outside. Their horses, tethered to the rail, tossed their heads, welcoming their owners. Their manes and tails flowed in the light breeze. All the matting from the rain had been combed out and their coats glistened in the morning light.

A boy about fifteen years of age stood near his father, the innkeeper. Ari reached into his pocket and paid them both. *Meta probably had no coins with her,* Ari thought. *This man was more than kind to take care of Meta and Anna.* "This is for taking care of our loved ones." The innkeeper graciously accepted the payment.

Journey in the Waiting

Farther down the trail, Benjamin exclaimed, "Ari, there's the group of rocks!"

"Good eyes, Benjamin," Ari noted. "I don't see as well as I use to. There's a village not far from here. We will stop and ask about Meta and Anna."

When the men stopped at the inn, sharp pains invaded Ivar's gut. He remembered that same feeling while he was in Herrgott when Falke had been following him. "What are You telling me, God?" he softly muttered.

Johann was the first one in the door. "Have you seen a woman traveling by herself with a baby yesterday?"

"No," the innkeeper replied, "the rain encouraged many travelers to stop for food and shelter, but none of them had a baby."

"Was there a woman traveling alone?" Johann continued.

"No," the innkeeper replied again, "only one woman was here, and she was with her husband."

"What color was her hair?" Benjamin asked, who had been quietly listening.

"Golden color…her hair was golden color."

Benjamin's heart sank. "Meta's hair is brown."

Life drained from Johann's face. Looking at his father, he asked, "Where are they?"

"She didn't stop here. We'll keep going." Turning to the innkeeper, Ari gritted his teeth and took a deep breath. "Thank you for the information. I want to purchase three loaves of bread." Tearing the bread in half, he gave each of his fellow riders something to eat. "Meta's smart. She decided to ride on and make it to the next village. Let's go."

At the next village, no one had seen Meta or a baby. The searchers rode on.

The sun dipped below the tree line, taking its brilliant illumination with it. The reluctant searchers stopped for the night. "Tomorrow, we'll be in Geir," Benjamin announced. He pressed his hand over his heart. A tightening pressure gripped his chest, and he gasped for air. "Why can't we find traces of Meta's journey?"

Johann slumped into a chair and stared at the floor. His faith waned. Magnus and Ivar sat on each side of their brother and put their hand on Johann's back. Johann drew a deep breath and envisioned holding his baby daughter.

Chapter 4

Geir

The dark morning sky resembled the outlook of finding Meta and Anna: bleak. Gradually, rays of daybreak illuminated the distant path and surrounding trees. Johann rubbed his neck, hoping to relieve the tension. Magnus and Ivar arched their aching backs. Benjamin just hung his head. Ari watched all of them while he tried to find a softer spot on his saddle. By midday, they would arrive at their destination.

Even though this was Johann's first trip past his hometown, the scenery held no interest to him. Focusing his mind on the whereabouts of his daughter, he prayed constantly during the trip. Ari watched his son while rubbing the locket under his shirt. *I need to give this locket back to Johann. He needs it now.*

Benjamin led them to his sister-by-marriage's house. With high hopes, he raised his clinched hand and knocked. Minna opened the door. "Benjamin, what a great surprise! Where's Meta?"

Benjamin slumped to the ground. He looked up to Minna with piercing eyes. "Meta's not here?"

"No. She never comes without you. Where is she?"

Benjamin looked at Johann and just slowly shook his head. Johann wanted to collapse to the ground. He looked at the sky and yelled, "Lord Jesus, help us!"

Minna's husband, Tomas, heard him and ran to the door. He led everyone into the house and seated them in the cooking room. His son tended the horses.

D Marie

Minna and Tomas served the group a warm drink and hot stew. Benjamin and the others looked at the food and moved their plates away. Minna and Tomas instinctively knew the men had horrible news.

Slowly, Benjamin rubbed his thumb over his finger while relating all of the events that had transpired during the last three days from the time the hawk guards had attacked to following Meta's tracks and losing them in the mud. Everyone hung their heads, all but Tomas.

"You found one inn where Meta stopped for food, but after that there were no tracks or visible signs of her passing through. Is that correct?" Tomas asked.

"Yes," Benjamin replied.

"Describe the area between the two inns."

"It's by the group of rocks," Benjamin began. Then a smile appeared on his face. He looked at Ari and exclaimed, "The arrow rocks! The other path!"

"That's it!" Ari yelled.

"What's it?" Johann asked.

"Meta went down the other path by the arrow rocks," Ari replied. "We have been going the wrong way."

"Thank you, Tomas!" Benjamin exclaimed.

"Let's finish this food," Johann said. "Suddenly, I'm hungry. Then, let's go."

"Your horses are being fed right now," Tomas said. "You'll all be ready at the same time."

"I'll pack up some food for you and Meta," Minna offered. "I have some milk for the baby."

Johann's shoulders slumped forcing a puff of air out of his lungs. "Thank You, Lord. Lead us to Anna and Meta."

After emptying his bowl, Ari picked up his bread. "Let's eat our bread on the way. We need to go."

Benjamin embraced his wife's sister and his brother-by-marriage. "Thank you for your help. You have given us new hope."

Journey in the Waiting

On the way out of town, Johann asked, "Papa, when was the last time you were on that other path?"

"It's been many years. The trail did not go very far, and I haven't heard of anyone talking about it."

"We need to check each village as we backtrack to see if anyone has seen them," Benjamin said.

"I agree," said Magnus. "Meta may have turned around and is heading this way."

"Done," said Ivar. "Let's pick up the pace."

Heading south, the group scanned the roadway, looking for any signs of Meta and Anna. Unfortunately, the sunlight diminished once again.

"Let's stay at a different inn for the night. Perhaps, we should ask the local villagers if they had seen our loved ones," Ari suggested. They all agreed and fanned out in each and every village, but none of the villagers had seen the missing woman and child.

That night, Johann got down on his knees and prayed, "Father in Heaven, I praise Your Holy Name. Your Kingdom is over all kingdoms. I do not understand why we cannot find my daughter and Meta, but let Your Kingdom and Your will be done here as it is in Heaven. I ask for You to supply our needs. Especially, supply the needs of Meta and Anna. Be with Tea while she is waiting for all of us to return with her baby. Lord, even though I am Yours, I still sin. Forgive me of my sins, and I forgive those who have sinned against me, even Falke and all of his group."

Johann paused for a moment, took a deep breath, and continued to pray, "If someone has harmed my daughter, I forgive them, too. Lead us away from temptation and deliver us from evil. For Yours is the power and the glory forever and ever. Amen."

Peace descended upon Johann. It enveloped him in complete tranquility. He laid down and immediately went to sleep.

Early the next morning, the sound of someone knocking on his door woke Johann up. "Wake up sleepy head," the voice commanded.

Johann got up and gathered his belongings. He looked up. "Thank You, Lord. I know You have my daughter in Your hands as well as Meta. I don't know the why, when, or how, but I know You are in control. I put my trust in You."

When Johann stepped out of the room, he sat down to the food on the table and waited for everyone to take their places. After the blessing of the food, Johann ate as though nothing was wrong. His brothers and father looked at him with amazement. Using his right hand, Johann pointed his index finger upward.

Magnus and Ivar repeated the action. Ari quickly followed. Benjamin raised his hands and looked up. "Help us, Lord."

Ari paid the innkeeper, and the others readied their horses. A cool breeze brushed across their heads carrying the earthy smell of the dirt road and an occasional scent of pine trees.

When they stopped for the night, Ari learned about the path by the arrow rock from the innkeeper. New settlements had sprung to existence along the path and it now went all the way to the sea.

"Be careful going down that path," the innkeeper warned. "There have been some young boys being mischievous to strangers. They like to jump out from the bushes and scare the horses."

"How long does it take to get to the sea?" Ari asked.

"If you leave at first light, you will be there before midday," the innkeeper replied. "It's not wise to travel by night because of those boys. They have been known to abscond with the horses if the riders fall off."

"Please, don't share this with the rest of the group," Ari implored. "I'll tell them in the morning." The innkeeper nodded and returned to his duties.

Everyone had a restful sleep that night except for Ari. In the morning, Ari informed the others about the boys. "We have to watch for any clue we may see on the path. If Meta lost the horse, that explains why she has not been quickly found."

"How will they eat?" Benjamin asked. His eyes begged for a positive answer.

Johann reached over and laid his hand on Benjamin's shoulder. "Benjamin, the Lord will provide."

Johann had more reason to be concerned. *Babies need milk*, he thought. *"Will the milk they received at the inn still be enough until they get help?*

Benjamin laid his hand on top of Johann's and said, "Johann, when two or more gather in prayer, the Lord promises to be there."

"That is true. Everyone, let's pray, then ride on."

My son is a leader that his family, friends, and subjects will respect. Just like my horses in training. Well done, Son, Ari thought.

All five of the searchers scoured the path. It had been four nights since the rain. New hoofprints appeared in the drying mud. They kept pressing on.

"Look, over there!" Benjamin shouted. Near the edge of the path lay a pile of cloth. A broken branch partially hid it.

"It looks like the cloak that Meta was wearing." Benjamin jumped off his horse and examined the garment. "No!" he screamed.

Benjamin ran his fingers through a rip in the back of the damp hood. Traces of blood appeared on his hand. The men feverishly looked everywhere but found no more clues.

"No weapon formed against me will prosper!" Johann declared.

"That's your scripture, Benjamin," Ari reminded his friend. "You said that when we passed Falke Castle, remember? We're on the right track. Let's go!"

A few rugged homes dotted the path. The men stopped at each structure, asking the same questions about Meta and Anna. No one had seen them. They came upon a small settlement, the beginning of a future village.

The shopkeeper eyed the group entering his store, hoping to make a sale. Johann approached him first. "Have you seen a woman traveling alone with a baby?"

"No," he replied somewhat disappointed that this group were not customers. Eyeing their dejected looks, he continued to talk. "But there was a man traveling with a woman and a baby." All eyes turned and landed on the shopkeeper. The shopkeeper's eyes drifted from one man to the next, trying to assess the situation.

"What did the woman look like?" Benjamin asked.

"She had brown hair and had a terrible cut in her scalp," the man replied with a slightly nervous tone in his voice. "I had to stitch it up."

"She's alive!" Benjamin exclaimed, leaning his shoulder on the wall.

"Do you know her?" the man asked.

Straightening up, Benjamin replied, "She's my wife!"

"Was the baby okay?" Johann intently asked.

"Yes," the man answered, relaxing a little. "A sweet little girl, and she was very hungry. I had to give her goat's milk, and she took it right away. I even got to hold her when her mother laid her aching head down."

"Thank you, Lord," Johann replied propping his back against the wall.

"Where are they now?" Ari asked.

"That's a good question," the man replied. "The man with her tried to find out if anyone recognized the woman. No one knew her or her baby. We asked her where she was from, but she couldn't utter a word. She couldn't use a quill and paper, either. She seemed dazed and confused. The only thing she could do was take care of that baby."

The shopkeeper paused still assessing the groups' reaction. Then he continued, "The gentleman that found them was hoping someone would be looking for them," the man continued. "All three of them stayed here for two nights. When no one came, he started to leave, but she clung to his arm. He didn't want to abandon the woman and her baby, so he allowed them to stay with him. I don't think he was from around here either."

"What makes you think that way?" Benjamin asked.

"He had an accent different from ours," the man noted.

"Which way did he go on the path?" Ivar asked.

"They went east. Keep following the path," the man replied.

"How far until we get to the sea?" Magnus asked.

"You're very close. It's just over that hill," the shopkeeper replied pointing to the rise in the land farther on down the path. This is the last settlement before you get to the coast.

"Let's go!" Benjamin yelled as he exited the door.

"Thank you for your help," Johann told the man. "I want to pay you for taking care of the woman and baby."

"The man took care of everything," the shopkeeper replied. "There's no debt."

The men quickly rode down the path, thinking this was the only path to the sea. If Meta and the baby come back down this road, they would be seen. Everyone was overjoyed, except

Ivar. He grabbed his midsection. That terrible feeling entered his gut again.

The smell of salt saturated the air making it relaxing to ride in. "We're almost there," Benjamin proclaimed riding in front of everyone.

A vast body of water came into view. A few buildings of various sizes stood a short distance from the water's edge. Crates and barrels were stacked up near the buildings. Two rowboats rested on the shoreline near a narrow dock.

The searchers went into the largest building and asked about Meta and Anna. "We saw them," one of the workers said. "The woman was very protective of her baby and wouldn't let anyone pull the blanket back to see her child."

"She never talked, but you could tell she was not happy with us," the proprietor of the shop said. "She stayed very close to the man with her."

"Where are they now?" Johann asked.

The proprietor pointed toward the water. "They left by sea two days ago."

Everyone's heart sank. Despair covered Benjamin's face and rendered him mute.

"Did he leave his name?" Ari asked.

"Yes, he did," the proprietor said. "He pointed to himself and said a name. I could not understand his accent very well. He's not from Christana. He pointed to the woman's head and kept repeating the word *arzt*. I don't know what that means. He said other things, but I just nodded, pretending I understood."

"What was his name?" Ari asked.

The proprietor cast his gaze toward the ground. "I don't remember."

"Did the man come this way before?" Johann intently asked.

"Yes," the man replied, looking up. "About three and a half weeks ago, he landed by a ship that was sailing north. He borrowed one of my horses and left a security for it. When he returned, he bought passage for another ship heading south. He returned my horse, and I returned his security. All three boarded and left."

"Did he mention where he was going?" Johann pressed on.

"He may have," the man replied, "but I couldn't understand his accent."

"What about the baby? What is she going to drink?" asked Magnus.

"The gentleman bought my goat," answered the proprietor with a positive tone in his voice.

As Ivar listened to the conversation, a sense of peace flooded his inner being and dispelled his queasy gut. He looked at Magnus' downcast face. Ivar turned around and looked at Johann. A slightly comforting look spread over his face. When the two brothers' eyes met, they smiled.

"Can you feel it, Johann?" Ivar asked.

"Yes," Johann replied, "God has His hand on this."

"What are you talking about?" Benjamin demanded.

"Benjamin," Johann began, "Meta was seriously hurt. This man recognized it. It doesn't sound like he wanted to take her with him, but she wanted to stay by his side. He must know someone that can help her. *Arzt* means physician in the Herrgott language. He's traveling south to take Meta to a physician. We don't know why he came here, but I trust God that He is going to return our loved ones to us safe and sound. Stefan the Younger said 'Anna is safe' right before he passed on. We now know both are safe, and Meta is going to get medical treatment for her head injury."

Johann turned to the proprietor and asked, "When does the next ship leave heading south?"

"They usually come every two weeks. It should be here in twelve days."

"How will we know when Meta and Anna return?" Benjamin moaned.

"There's a surplus of guards at the palace. Some of those guards could be assigned here at this post." Johann replied.

"It's time the outlining villages and settlements have better protection."

"You must be a man of authority. Thank you," the proprietor acknowledged. "Perhaps you can do something about those boys who scare people off their horses."

Benjamin clinched his fists. "Maybe that's what caused Meta to get the gash in her head."

"Do you know anything about these boys," Johann asked.

"They have no families or homes," the man said in a soft voice. "They are homeless. If they catch a horse, I suspect they sell it for food. They don't bring the horses here."

"Was the woman still wearing a ring?" Benjamin asked relaxing his fingers.

"Yes," the man replied, "I thought she was the wife of the foreigner."

"She's my wife. Her name is Meta," Benjamin replied.

"I'm so sorry," the man said looking at Benjamin. "Even though your wife was injured, she was taking good care of your baby."

Benjamin started to reply, but Johann grabbed his arm and interrupted. "If this man, Meta, and the baby return, let them know we are looking for them. They are from Christana. I know King Albert very well. I will talk to him about getting guards here immediately."

"Thank you, sirs," the proprietor replied. "My dock has only been here a few months. I'm hoping to grow a settlement here for seafaring trade with other countries. And I'll be watching for your family."

Returning to their horses, the group of men stared at the open sea. One by one, they drew a deep breath and pulled their reins, guiding their horses back to the path. Everyone departed with some glimmer of hope. Each one contemplated what they were going to tell their loved ones when they return to Christana.

Chapter 5

Compassion

P*lop, plop, plop. Plop, plop, plop.* The rhythmic noise of the horses' hoofs pounded the dirt path, offering a melancholy sound for soul searching. Johann edged his horse next to his father. Magnus motioned to Ivar and they rode behind the other two. Benjamin never noticed. He continued to hang his head, seldom looking up.

"Father," Johann began, "I need advice."

"I'm here, Son."

"We'll be home before nightfall. Telling Tea and the family will be hard enough, but what should we tell the townsfolk?"

"I've been thinking of this, too," Ari replied. "Maybe, it's better to tell them nothing for the moment."

As they got closer to the arrow rock, a boy came out of the woods with a horse. His clothes indicated that they had not been washed, maybe never. Dirt and grim covered his hands and parts of his face. Mud stuck to his crude shoes that had straw in them for extra warmth. The boy approached Johann and asked, "Kind sir, I found this horse in the woods. No one claims it. Would you like to buy it?"

Benjamin perked up. His eyes narrowed as he scrutinized the horse. "Let me examine it first."

When Benjamin recognized the tracks in the dusty path, he knew it was the horse Meta had ridden. He moved closer to the boy and grabbed his arm.

"Ow!" the boy yelled. "You're hurting me."

The other four men dismounted and stood in a circle around the boy. The child wrapped his arms around his chest and started to cry.

"Please don't hurt me," the boy begged trying to pull away from Benjamin's grip. "I didn't steal the horse. I found it walking around the woods."

"Are there others with you?" Benjamin yelled.

"Yes, but they're scattered by now."

"Where do you stay?" Benjamin continued his questioning.

"Anywhere we feel safe," the boy answered with his head down, giving up on his escape. "Never in the same place for very long. No one wants us around."

Benjamin loosened his grip and let the child step back away from him. The boy bumped into Johann. Fear gripped his thoughts. *I'm surrounded.*

"Did you see a woman on this horse?" Benjamin asked in a calmer voice.

"No," the boy replied. "I found the horse yesterday. Are you missing a horse? You can have it. Just let me go."

"Young man," Johann began in a warm and gentle voice, "would you like to ride with us and see a big town? I could use a person of your ability to take care of horses."

The boy's eyes lit up. "Can I sleep in the barn with the horses? Do I get food to eat every day? I'm a fast learner."

"Whoa," Johann interrupted. "Let's see if you will like the job first. If you do, we'll take care of the other requirements."

"If it has a roof, I'll like it."

All five men let out a deep sigh. Johann turned his head to regain his composure.

Ari spoke up. "Well, boy, if you are going to work with horses, you need to mount up and ride this one."

"You mean it?"

Johann nodded. Benjamin offered a slight smile. Ari helped the boy into the saddle. A few hours later, Christana came into view. When the guards saw six riders coming to the palace, they smiled and sent servants to get the royal family. Tea frantically searched the group but didn't see Meta. Her body trembled. Her eyes pleaded with Johann.

The weary riders dismounted. Benjamin's son ran into his father's arms. The boy from the woods stared at the interior courtyard. His bulging eyes scanned the palace grounds, absorbing the strange surroundings. Ari, Magnus, and Ivar stood quietly behind the boy.

Johann took Tea into his arms. Tears ran down her face as he told her about Anna and Meta. She laid her head on Johann's shoulder, sobbing uncontrollably and causing her whole body to shake. Helplessness overwhelmed Johann. He wanted to weep with her, but gritting his teeth, he momentarily held his breath and remained strong for his wife.

Maria bit her lip as she watched her daughter go through agony. Blood started to seep out, and she relaxed her mouth. Albert's tightly clinched fists turned white. Waiting to comfort his daughter seemed like eternity.

Remorse overwhelmed Stefan. Temptation flooded his mind and nagged him, saying, "It's all your fault. All of these events are happening, because you didn't do your responsibilities as a father years ago."

He turned his head away from his family and quietly addressed the thoughts, "My Lord convicts me when I do wrong. He doesn't condemn me. This is not from God. Go away in the name of Jesus." The harassing thoughts immediately left.

Tea took several deep breaths and regained her composure. She dried her eyes. Tea took another deep breath and said, "Thank You, Lord Jesus." Looking at Benjamin she nodded to his son and asked, "Does he know?"

Benjamin sadly shook his head.

"May I talk to Josef about this?"

Looking at Tea with grateful eyes, Benjamin nodded.

"Josef," Tea called to the little boy, "I need some help. Will you help me?"

"Yes, Ma'am," the boy replied with a bewildered look.

"My little girl needed some medicine in a faraway town. Your mama was kind and offered to take Anna and stay with her. I miss her and your mother dearly. Could you be brave with me as we both wait for them to return?"

Josef eyes brightened as he smiled. "Of course, Ma'am. Papa tells me I am a brave boy all the time. We can be brave together. Papa, you can be brave with us while Mama is gone?"

Benjamin stared at Tea. Tears stung his eyes. *This is a wonderful way to explain the absence of Josef's mother and baby Anna. My son can be brave and not be scared.*

"Yes, Son," Benjamin replied, chocking back his emotions. "We can all be brave together."

"How about the boy over there?" Josef asked, pointing to the other child. "Is he here to be brave, too?"

Tea walked over to the young boy. She sensed there was something wrong, otherwise this child would not be here. Tea picked up his hand and asked him, "Can you be brave with us?"

"Yes, Ma'am," the boy responded. "I have to be brave every day."

"Why do you have to be brave every day?" Tea asked.

"I don't have a mama or papa anymore. I don't have a home either."

Tea looked at Johann. He knew that look and nodded. She returned a grateful smile. Looking at the young boy, she asked, "What is the name of this very brave boy?"

"Daniel. It's the only thing I have left from my parents."

"Can he stay in my room?" Josef asked, tugging on Tea's dress.

Tea looked at her parents and Benjamin. They all nodded. She walked a step closer to Daniel, leaned over, and hugged the young boy. The tenseness in his muscles relaxed, and he put his trust in the first adult since he had lost his parents.

Tea took her hands and cupped them on Daniel's face. "Josef, can be a little fussy with bath time, could you help us? Afterward, it will be time for the evening meal."

"Yes, Ma'am!" he replied with a big smile. "I will help you with anything you ask."

Josef took Daniel's hand and led him to the bathing chamber. Tea rushed to her parents and wrapped her arms around both. "Someone is providing a safe home for my daughter. We can do the same for Daniel. The Lord provides."

Albert and Maria gazed at their daughter. "Tea, we're so proud of you. Despite the pain you're enduring right now, you're pouring out your love on this child," Albert said.

"Papa," Tea replied, "The Lord is my Healer. If I didn't have Him in my life, I would not be thinking of the needs of His people. I will cling to Him while I wait for my baby."

Silence fell over everyone while they contemplated those words. Maria took hold of her daughter's hands. "Tea, it's every parents' desire for their children to love the Lord and serve Him. God will bless this awful situation and make something good come from it."

"Thank you, Mama. If it wasn't for your and Papa's examples, I may not have known about the love of Jesus. Now, we can show that love to Daniel."

"Speaking of Daniel," Maria interjected, "let's go check on our two boys. They will be finished soon. We need some new clothes for Daniel, too. Albert, let's have a big meal this evening. Ivar, Magnus, please bring Petra and Angela for our evening meal. Tonight, Daniel will be surrounded by family."

"While you're preparing the lads, I will bring Johann and Ari up-to-date with your vision." Albert winked. The corners of Maria's mouth pulled up in return. Lacing her arm in Tea's, they walked inside the palace.

After the meal was over, Tea and Benjamin led the two boys to their room. The servants had already placed an additional bed in the room for Daniel.

"I get to sleep here?" Daniel asked. "I thought I would sleep with the horses."

"I can ask them if they have room, but they do snore," Benjamin replied with a grin. Tea rolled her eyes and let go of a soft giggle.

"I don't want to bother them," Daniel replied. "I'll stay here, but can I work with them tomorrow?"

"We'll see," Benjamin replied. "First we have to find the real owner of the horse you found, because I took it without permission."

Daniel's jaw dropped and looked at Benjamin with disbelief. Josef opened his eyes wide and stared at his father. Tea came to the rescue. "The owner was understanding. We told him a few days ago that we needed to borrow his horse. Before we return the horse, we need to curry him."

"May I do it?" Daniel asked. "I love being around horses."

"Certainly, now it's time to get ready for bed," Tea responded.

Benjamin helped his son get dressed. He listened while Josef said his prayers. When he mentioned his mother's name, Josef asked, "Lord grant Momma and baby Anna safe journey and help them find the medicine."

Johann walked in. He watched Tea tenderly help the boy get ready for bed. Once the lad was tucked in, he looked up at

Journey in the Waiting

Tea and said, "Good night, Ma'am, and thank you." He looked at Johann and said, "Good night and thank you, Lord Jesus."

Tea and Johann raised their eyebrows. Tilting his head, Johann asked, "Why did you call me Lord Jesus?"

"That's what Ma'am called you. I thought that was your name."

"Sir will be a good name for now. Lord Jesus is a name that belongs to someone else. She was talking to Him. Would you like to learn about Jesus?"

"Does He like children?" Daniel asked.

"He especially loves children!" Johann responded.

"Yes, I want to learn about Jesus."

Johann walked over to Daniel's bed and began to teach him about his Heavenly Father and Jesus. Tea and Benjamin, still hurting from their loss, took a small measure of contentment seeing this orphaned boy learning about God. Silently they walked away and found the rest of the family.

"Benjamin," Ari said waving to him, "we need your help."

"Where's Johann?" Albert asked.

"He's teaching Daniel about someone he doesn't know about," Benjamin replied with a soft smile. "Jesus."

Ari sighed. *My son is sharing the Good News in the midst of missing his daughter.* Ari cleared his throat and redirected his thoughts. "We need to devise our best course of action. Since I know the northern area the best, I suggest that I travel to the villages there and find out who this gentleman visited. Benjamin, since you know the language of this man better than I do, you could take the next ship sailing south and start looking in the ports along the coast."

Benjamin's heart pounded harder. Heavy breathing caused his chest to raise up and down. Perhaps he could find their trail. "This is a great plan. I can find out how many ports the ship goes to and map them out. I'll ask questions just like you will be asking. I just don't want to wait and hope they'll return."

"Neither does any one of us," Albert interjected. "I want to go, but I'm needed here."

As they discussed the journeys, Johann walked into the room. He agreed with the plan. "I will go with you, Benjamin." Albert reached out his hand and laid it on Johann's shoulder and whispered in his ear. Johann pursed his lips and gave a slight nod.

With half closed eyes, Johann said, "Father, I will go with you instead. As we travel through the villages, I can also see firsthand what the people have and need. Since we came through the area already in common clothes, I suggest we do it again."

Ari slightly cocked an eyebrow but nodded in agreement.

Benjamin drew in a deep breath. Albert noticed and said, "Benjamin, spend all of the time you want with your son. Let him enjoy these days with you. Daniel is a Godsend. He will keep Josef occupied while you are gone. You will not be searching alone. I will personally select three guards to travel with you. All of you will be wearing common clothing. Our guards' uniforms will be out of place in Herrgott."

Ivar laid his hand on Johann's shoulder. "Johann, I can't imagine the pain you are going through. Magnus and I are right next door in the church if you need us."

"You know we will be praying for you and your family," Magnus said. "We are here for you, Brother."

"Son," Ari began, "if there is one thing that I have learned about being a Christian is that if God is for us who can be against us. We will find your daughter." Ari's arms wrapped around his youngest son. "Now, it's time to take Petra and Angela home. Good night, Johann."

After Petra and her cousin gave their farewells, she thought about what they could do to help. "Let's make Ari and Johann a new banner."

"Perfect. It can give them comfort on their next journey," Angela replied.

Petra laced her arm around her cousin's arm, drawing her closer. "Let's keep it a surprise until they leave."

Chapter 6

New Beginnings

A grimace appeared on Gunther's face as he approached the mares' stable, thinking about the captives inside. It was just yesterday that those men had attacked the palace.

The torch light flickered and offered a little illumination for the attending guards. Recognizing Gunther, they nodded and stepped aside. Peering into the doorway, Gunther spotted his target. Pursing his lips, he reached in and tapped Gabriel on his shoulder. Startled, the young man threw up his hands to grab Gunther's arm. Just as fast, he came to his senses and quickly pulled his arms back. Gunther raised his index finger to his mouth and motioned for him to be quiet. "Gabriel," he whispered, "gather your things."

Without delay, Gabriel got up and followed the horse-trainer to the waiting group of mounted guards. First light revealed Gunther's extended hand with some food wrapped in a cloth. Gabriel gratefully accepted anything that he received. He had no guarantee that Gunther would take him on this journey. *Why should I be trusted?* he thought. *Just a few hours ago, I was part of the attacking force on this palace.*

Determined to be compliant, Gabriel remained on his best behavior with the palace guards. He knew their trust had to be earned and that his conduct would be closely watched. He never talked unless he was spoken to first.

"We'll go to the attackers' camp first," Gunther ordered. "Gabriel, lead the way."

D Marie

As they rode out, Gunther pondered on Gabriel's information, wondering why there were no guards at the campsite only supplies and a wagon. At least fifteen guards still remained at the castle, and they were younger, untrained men. The older guards had gone with Falke. Wanting to make a strong show of force to the castle guards, Gunther was taking forty Christanan guards with him.

Upon reaching the invaders' campsite, the garrison of guards found supplies and the charred remains of a large campfire. Gunther motioned for the guards to gather the supplies and hitch up two horses to the wagon.

As a precaution, four guards accompanied Gabriel at all times. He wasn't bound with ropes, but his movements were limited. Two nights later, they stood in front of their destination, the Hawk Man's castle.

An immense gate made of iron bars stood in front of massive wooden doors. The hawk flag fluttered in the wind. The ominous castle deterred unwelcomed strangers.

Peering over the ramparts, Falke's castle guards noticed the tunics of the Christana guards but were not alarmed. After all, Falke and their fellow guards had been asked to go to Christana to protect the royal family. These guards were never told about the lie of rebellion.

Looking at Gunther, Gabriel's eyes asked for permission to address the castle guards. Gunther understood and nodded. "Guards of Falke Castle, Falke lied to us. All of his guards are prisoners, and Falke is dead. We're here to undo the evil he has done to this castle and to you."

The guards all withdrew from the ramparts. After a few moments, the hawk flag came tumbling down the castle wall. Several startled horses backed up and neighed loudly in protest. Next, the tunics bearing the hawk emblem came tumbling down the wall. For the last gesture, the iron portcullis slowly rose up and the thick wooden doors swung open.

Gunther and his men cautiously guided their horses into the inside of the castle. A pile of weapons rested in the middle of the courtyard, their young owners standing quietly next to the pile.

"Are all the guards here?" Gabriel asked the frightened group in the Herrgott language.

"Yes," one of the hawk guards replied.

"Please don't hurt us," another begged. "We didn't know. We're sorry."

"Men don't talk like that," Gunther muttered understanding their language, "Children do."

"What is your age?" Gunther asked one of the castle guards.

"Sixteen, Sir," the boy replied with a quivering lip.

"Who is older than sixteen?" Gunther asked the group. No one responded. "Who is younger than sixteen?" Over half of the boys raised their hands.

Gunther turned his head to regain his composure for he hadn't conquered rebellious men; he had found frighten boys. "Lord help me. What should I do?" His eyes scanned the interior walls, noting stairs, windows, and doors. "Guards, I need to become familiar with the castle, and I need time to contemplate the fate of the captives."

A loud gasp erupted from the boys.

Gunther realized he had been talking in Herrgott, but it was too late. Addressing the guards, he spoke in their language. "Watch over the boys and try to make them as comfortable as possible."

"Sir, we know very little of the language they speak," one guard pointed out. "But we will try."

Gunther faced the boys, motioning his hands downward he spoke in a calm voice. "Please, sit quietly until I call for you." He shook his head as he continued. "You will not be harmed."

Turning to Gabriel, Gunther beckoned him to come. "Guide me through the castle. Hold back nothing." Gabriel nodded. He showed Gunther and five other guards all the rooms and secret passageways. When the tour was over, the group returned to the dining hall and sat down.

"Gabriel," Gunther began, "how well do you know these boys?"

"When new recruits first arrive, Falke insisted they forget about their past and focus on their future of the good life here at the castle. Information about our families was not shared. We're one family at the castle. I don't know anything about the boys' real families."

"What would you do with these boys?"

"They're scared, and they need to be talked to calmly in a nonthreatening place. Perhaps one child at a time talks with one interrogator. See what their thoughts are on this situation. So far, they have done nothing wrong except to follow Falke's deception. Where their allegiance is now is the unknown factor."

"Where's your allegiance now, Gabriel?"

"That's difficult to say."

"Why is it difficult?" Gunther probed further.

"I'm from Herrgott. You're from Christana. I know my city, but I do not know yours."

"Gabriel, Herrgott is my birthplace, too."

Gabriel's eyes lit up. "I pledge my allegiance to King Stefan, his family, and those who represent them."

"Good. I'll have the boys brought up to this room. You can reassure them when they get here not to be afraid. They'll not be harmed. I will question each boy individually in a separate room while you and the other boys remain in the dining hall."

Gunther headed for the courtyard. He appointed several guards to occupy the ramparts and instructed them to wave on any boats traveling on the converging rivers. The remaining guards brought the boys to the dining hall. Some of the guards were sent to the cooking room to prepare the next meal.

Gabriel motioned for the boys to sit. After talking to the boys, the frightened looks on their faces started to relax a little. When Gunther took one of the boys out of the room, the other boys whispered to one another. "I think we'll not be hurt," one of them said with a sigh of relief. The others smiled hopefully.

By the time Gunther finished with the last boy, the meal was ready to be served. The boys offered to set the table. They quietly retrieved and laid out all the necessary plates and utensils.

Gunther sat down and asked the Lord's blessing on the food. The boys looked at each other with puzzled looks. When he was finished, Gunther announced, "Gentlemen, enjoy your meal."

One of the boys raised his hand to speak. Gunther nodded. "What was the purpose of saying those words before we eat?"

All the boys looked intently at Gunther. "This food comes from God's Earth. We thank Him for the meal to show Him respect and honor. It's another way to acknowledge our faith in God."

"Can we learn about God, too?" the curious boy asked.

"Who else wants to learn about God?" All the boys raised their hands.

"Yes," Gunther replied, "you can learn about God."

Since the boys' sleeping quarters were close together, the Christanan guards could easily monitor them. That night, Gunther contemplated the information he'd gleaned from the young Falke guards. Some of them regretted leaving home, but they didn't know if their parents would let them return. Some of the boys had no home to return to. They wanted to stay.

During the morning meal, Gunther made his announcement. "Gentlemen, I will return to Christana tomorrow. King Stefan has given a new name to this castle: Taulbe. This will be your home until I return. The Head Guard will be your leader. All of you will continue your regular routines."

"Gabriel," Gunther continued, "would you teach the guards the procedures for collecting the tolls for the river passage? All boat and ship captains need to be informed of the new ownership and be assured that reasonable fees will be charged by order of the King of Herrgott."

"Yes," Gabriel replied, "it will be my pleasure to help."

"Good," Gunther said. "We can discuss the old and current fees while we walk to the river."

Gunther contemplated what Stefan would want to charge—less than Falke had for sure. Watching a log drift by, he turned to Gabriel. "Let's lower the fee by one coin until I confer with King Stefan. He will decide the final price."

Gabriel nodded and kept his thoughts to himself. *Falke always overcharged, and the poor captains had no recourse but to pay his price. Our new master will be more just.*

The moving water captivated Gunther's attention. Gabriel watched him and asked, "Do you like to fish, Sir?" Gunther frowned. Gabriel lowered his head. "Excuse me, Sir."

"It's alright, Gabriel. I'm not used to hearing myself called sir."

"What would be a good title, ss-," Gabriel caught himself and stopped.

"Gunther, would be enough."

"Do you like to fish, Gunther?"

Journey in the Waiting

"Yes, I used to fish as a child near the bridge in Herrgott."

"You must be careful in these waters. The convergence of the two rivers create dangerous currents under the surface. They can pull you down and keep you there."

Gunther stared at the rocks near the shore and spied the perfect skimmer. He picked up a flat stone, gripped it with his fingers, and flipped it across the water. The stone skipped the water surface ten or more times before it sank. Gabriel's eyes widened. Gunther grinned and tilted his head a little. "I practiced while waiting for the fish to bite."

The following day, Gunther started his journey back to Christana. He took a few of the guards with him and the youngest boy from the castle, the one who had asked about God. Upon arriving at the palace, King Albert and King Stefan anxiously called upon him to give a report about Taulbe Castle. Gunther was eager to hear about the baby and Meta.

"Well done, Gunther. You have handled this situation well," Stefan said. "I will lower the passage on the river by another two coins. I want to encourage more trade from the different villages and kingdoms. Now, what do we do with the boys at the castle."

"What are your thoughts, Gunther?" Albert asked.

"I pondered on this on the journey here. I suggest we take the boys back to Herrgott that have families there and see if they can be reunited. If they can, we'll check up on the boys with some type of supervision and monitoring. Perhaps, they will make wiser choices in the future."

"The boys without family," Gunther continued, "should be given an opportunity to stay at Taulbe Castle as apprentices or join the other prisoners. If they stay at Taulbe, we can help them grow up."

"Wise thinking," Stefan replied. "Let's implement your plan. From the looks of the boy you brought back, we have a responsibility to give him and the other boys a better upbringing than what they had so far."

"Gunther," Albert asked, "If you had more guards, could you take some of the prisoners here to Taulbe Castle? We need better housing for them, and they need training."

"Yes," Gunther replied, "I have explored the whole castle, and there's plenty of room. What would they be training for?"

Albert looked at Stefan and smiled. Stefan replied, "To build a bridge over the Vogel River. We have been questioning the captured men, and many of them have skills besides riding horses and carrying swords."

Gunther's eyes beamed. "Thank you. This will be a benefit for many people and for future generations. I have another suggestion."

"Please share," Stefan replied.

"There's a need for a road from Taulbe Castle to Christana. The current path is overgrown and tricky—no defined trail, low lying tree limbs, and bushes everywhere. The bridge will require materials from both sides of the Vogel River."

"Done," said Albert. "We can have the prisoners get started on it right away. We need a new name for them. What about detainees?"

"Good choice," Stefan replied. "It's our goal to detain them for only a short period of time. Then, they can be free."

"We will still have plenty of guards with them," Albert added. "The detainees will be using axes to chop down trees and other tools to clear a path. We don't want an uprising."

"When do you want me to return to Taulbe?" Gunther asked.

Stefan took in a deep breath. "After my son's funeral, Gunther. All of my family is here, so he will be buried in the palace burial ground. When it is my turn to go, I'll be buried next to him. I think he would have liked that. We have been waiting for you to return."

Gunther's jaw dropped. *I'm included in the families' time of mourning.* He stiffened up and regained his composure. "If there is anything else I can do, please let me know."

"There is one more thing," Albert replied. Gunther met Albert's eyes. "When Ari leaves, we have no idea how long he will be gone. He's the only one you have taught to work with the Edelrosses. Could you take them to Taulbe Castle and continue working with them there?"

"Yes!" Gunther replied loudly. "I can use the detainees' help, too. Perhaps, I can train some of them." A smiled spread across his face. He wanted to tell his horses right away that they were coming with him. "The courtyard is not as big as Christana's. I suggest that only the stallions go to Taulbe. The mares could stay here with their foals."

Albert placed his hand next to his face and covered his chin. "Good idea. I agree."

Rays of the morning sunlight streamed through the opened branches of the trees. A gentle breeze ruffled the leaves. Despite the warmth of the day, the traditional happy greetings had transformed into quiet stares and occasional nods of the head.

King Stefan had abandoned the traditional church service, choosing instead a private funeral for his son, Stefan the Younger, on the palace grounds. Magnus and Ivar nodded to the royal family when all was ready. Magnus momentarily clinched his squared jaw and started with a prayer.

When their loved one was laid to rest, everyone remained quiet for several minutes. The sun warmed their faces, and the flowers shared their sweet fragrance. A gentle breeze made another pass by the trees, creating a soft rustling noise with the leaves.

Finally, Stefan walked away. Albert and Maria followed together and then Johann and Tea. Magnus and Angela walked side by side, and Ivar walked with his betrothed, Petra. Ari laid his arm on Benjamin's shoulder while the boys followed.

Gunther walked alone. Watching everyone in front of him, he quietly muttered, "I pray that someday I'll have a family, but what woman would want to look at me?" He reached for his scar. It used to be a reminder of his hatred toward the Hawk Man. Now, it was a reminder of his salvation when he'd given that hatred to God.

Everyone shared the midday meal. The boy from the Taulbe Castle sat next to Daniel. It was the quietest meal the servants had ever witnessed. Even Daniel and Josef never spoke a word.

Suddenly, the young detainee boy looked at Ivar and asked, "Do you know the God that everyone prays to before they eat?"

Ivar, being caught off guard by the question, looked at the boy with puzzlement. Relaxing his eyes, he answered, "Yes, I do. May I help you learn about God?"

"I sure hope so," the boy replied. "I want to know, and my friends at the castle want to know."

Ivar looked at Petra. She smiled and winked at him. *What's that supposed to mean?* Ivar thought.

After the meal, Stefan asked Ivar to take a walk with him. Sensing Stefan may want some spiritual help, Ivar quickly accepted the invitation. He patted Petra on the hand and told her he would see her soon. She smiled and winked again.

As they strolled in the garden, Stefan asked, "Do you like horses?"

"Yes, I grew up working with them," Ivar replied.

"Do you like serving the Lord?" Stefan probed further.

"Yes, it's my life's calling to serve God and His people." Ivar scratched his head, wondering where this line of questions was leading.

"Would you like an opportunity to have both?" Stefan offered.

"That would be wonderful, but King Albert has plenty of caretakers for the horses."

"This job opportunity is not here in Christana. It's at Taulbe Castle. Gunther will be there with many detainees that do not know the Lord, and he's taking the Edelross stallions there to continue their training."

A faint smile appeared on Ivar's face. *Sharing the Gospel with unbelievers is what I was trained to do. Working with the Edelrosses is a rare opportunity and honor*, Ivar thought. Then, his smile disappeared.

Stefan noticed and said, "That castle has never had a woman's touch. Some of those detainees there are younger than sixteen and don't have parents. They could use a mother figure in their life." Then, Stefan slowly winked at him.

"I get it!" Ivar announced.

"Get what?" Stefan asked.

"Petra winked at me at the table when the boy spoke out. Then, she winked again when I left with you. She sensed something and was giving her approval."

"That's a special woman," Stefan noted.

"Stefan," Ivar began before pausing for a moment. "I can't take an unmarried woman there with all those detainees."

Stefan paused, raising his hand he cupped his chin. "What if she could take several female servants to help and keep her company. We can hire additional qualified maidens. That might tip the balance a little."

"How can this be?" Ivar asked. "I make a small sum as a minister."

"You will get two incomes, one for the Lord's work and one for training Albert's horses," Stefan continued. "Lodging and food are included. Everyone would be paid by the castle's income. I would imagine my son has a large amount of coins in the coffer already."

"You're very generous. I have to talk with Petra first."

"Of course. Let's send for her right now."

Petra came to the garden area and Stefan temporarily left so they could discuss their future. "Yes!" Petra replied.

Stefan smiled as her words sweetly floated in the air and landed in his ears. He waited a little longer for them to continue their talk before joining them.

"I can be closer to Herrgott and my family," Petra shared. "I can start my school about God with these boys. Can they read? I can start a school for that, too."

Ivar took Petra in his arms. His heart swelled with thoughts of how his true love was helping him to do the work he too loved.

Ivar and Petra agreed to postpone a wedding date. Finding Anna and Meta was more important than celebrating a marriage. They began the preparations for their new life in the castle and decided to join Gunther on his next trip to investigate their future home, taking three Edelrosses with them.

Chapter 7

Father and Son

Johann drummed his fingers on the arm of his chair. *Tap, tap, tap. Tap, tap, tap.* Staring at the various books sitting on the shelves, he contemplated his first trip north. "What clues did we miss? What information will we find this time?" he muttered. Turning his head toward the window, a heavy feeling started to invade his thoughts and hang over his head. Johann immediately discerned the unwanted pressure.

"Stop it," Johann yelled. "The Lord is my provider. He will lead us to my daughter."

Tea ears perked up. "What's going on, Johann?"

"Tea, let's pray. It's nearly time for the next ship to arrive, and I need prayer."

Reaching for Johann's hands, Tea began the prayer. "Father God, we come before You with our humble hearts. Open our eyes that we see Your will in this circumstance. Our daughter is missing and Meta is injured. We need Your provision and healing. Have mercy on us. In Your Name we pray, Jesus. Amen."

Johann slowly closed his eyes. Peace swept over his whole body. His body fully relaxed as he fellowshipped with God. The heavy feeling vanished.

Looking into his wife's eyes, Johann spoke, "Tea, I'm supposed to be the strong one for you. Thank you for your prayer."

"Johann, God wants us to support each other when we trust in Him. We don't know when or where, but we do know the Lord is faithful. We will take it one day at a time."

* * *

Petra and Angela waited for Ari to make his way into the cooking room. He noticed cute smiles on their faces and scrunched his eyebrows, making deep lines in his forehead.

Angela pointed to the table. Ari's eyes opened wide when he saw two identical banners that looked like his old one. "We made these for you and Johann," said Angela.

A tear rolled down Ari's cheek, and he wiped it off. "Thank you. This is perfect for our journey." Ari folded up his first banner his wife had once made and returned it to his Bible. It had proudly resided on Ari's saddle horn, but constant use had taken a toll, and it was frayed beyond repair. He looked up and said, "Your banner will always remind me of the Lord. Thank you, Johanna." He took the two new banners and headed for town.

A group of tethered horses trailed behind Ari. He didn't want to draw too much attention to their second search in this short period of time, so he suggested bringing some of his saddle broke horses to sell. Johann agreed. Ample opportunities for conversations would be provided when the villagers saw his horses.

Two wagons loaded up with supplies waited in the palace courtyard. The materials would become the beginning of a port village. Albert and his counselors had also discussed sending some of the detainees to help with the construction. Since there was not any proper housing, they had decided to wait. The searchers and the garrison of guards gave one last wave to those staying behind and headed for the palace gate.

Trotting down the path, Ari prayed, "Lord, help us on this journey. Lead us to the information we need to find Anna and Meta. In Your Name I pray. Amen."

When they arrived at the port landing, Ari spied the proprietor and galloped to his side. "Is there any news about Meta and Anna?"

The proprietor looked soulfully at Ari. "I haven't heard or seen anything about the woman and child." Johann and his father dropped their eyes and ventured toward the shoreline.

The guards had taken a different task and looked around the landing, assessing the best area to build their structure. When they found a good foundation, they started to rope off the area to lay out the dimensions of the building.

The proprietor noticed the new activity and beamed with delight at the thought of having the guards at his landing. *Now, I'll have protection for my business and customers.* Not sure of who was in charge, he decided to approach the oldest man there, Ari.

"I'm grateful for what the king is doing here," the proprietor said. "Please inform the king of my gratitude."

"I will," Ari replied.

"Would the king like to name this village in the making?" the proprietor asked. "Since you're looking for the two people, you could put their names together and call it Metanna."

Benjamin looked at Johann and gave him a faint smile. Johann nodded in acknowledgement. "I'll give the king your suggestion," Johann answered. "It's a good name. I hope he likes it."

The ship appeared in the distance. Benjamin and the three guards, who wore plain clothes, prepared to board. They watched a rowboat come to shore with a uniformed man sitting in the stern. The captain sized up his new passengers and cargo. "Gentlemen, I wish I could accommodate all of you, but there's not enough room for four men and four horses. I could accommodate one horse and one man or four men. But there may not be horses at the next port for all four of you to use."

Benjamin looked at Ari with a look of half despair and half frustration. He had planned to disembark at each port and search each village for clues. Four people would make the search faster.

"Go Benjamin," Ari told him, "and may the Lord be with you."

The guards walked over to Benjamin and gave him their coin pouches that King Albert had supplied for their traveling needs. Benjamin stared at the pouches, contemplating his journey. *Lord be with me. I'll be alone in a strange land.* Looking upward, peace enveloped him. "Thank You, Jesus. I'm not alone. You are with me."

Benjamin coaxed his horse to step into the water. He entered the rowboat, taking the stern seat and gently pulled the reins of his horse until the horse started to swim. The captain sat in the bow. Nearing the ship, the captain ordered his crew to swing the crane over the side of his ship for the swimming cargo. Deck hands jumped into the water and secured the riggings and sling around the middle of the horse. The bewildered animal thrashed his legs and head as he was hoisted up into the air and lowered into the cargo hold. Benjamin looked at his frightened friend. Climbing into the hold, he immediately began to soothe his companion with his voice and comforting touch.

After the ship departed, Ari and Johann prepared themselves to leave the seaport and head north. The proprietor walked up to them and bid his farewells. Then he remembered something. "The gentleman you were asking about, he must have been a man of means."

"Why do say that?" Ari asked.

"He was finely dressed for his travels. He didn't wear the common clothes we're wearing."

Ari and Johann both closed their eyes and took a deep breath. "This is a clue," Ari cried out. "Benjamin needs to know this!" Ari yelled and waved his arms from the shore, but the people on board just waved in return unable to understand any words.

Journey in the Waiting

With their horses in tow, the father and son planned to stop at every settlement, asking about the man with the heavy accent. Passing the arrow rock, Ari said, "I wish we–"

"Papa," Johann interrupted. "We didn't know. We can't punish ourselves. We'll find them. It's all in God's timing."

Briefly closing his eyes, Ari pondered on the opportunity of being there for Johann and being a part of his son's life. Approaching the first inn, he sighed, "Let's get something to eat and begin our search."

"Welcome," the innkeeper greeted them happily. "You two are back so soon."

"We have horses to sell," Ari replied. "Do you know of anyone who is in need of a saddle broke horse?"

"I wish I had one a few weeks ago," the innkeeper shared. "I had a finely dressed traveler who had a horse that was past his prime. I think he would have been interested in one of your horses."

Johann and Ari listened intently. Johann asked, "Perhaps, we might find him. Do you remember his name?"

"Yes," the innkeeper answered, "Wilhelm. It's the same as my father's name. That's easy for me to remember."

Johann did a quick look at his father and refocused on the innkeeper. "Do you know where we might find this man?"

"I don't know. He's not from around here. He had a heavy accent, and it was difficult to understand him. Odd fellow he was."

"Why do you say that? Ari asked.

"The look on his face, most unfriendly. After he finished his meal, he left."

Johann locked eyes with his father. "We're on the right path, Papa."

"Path?" questioned the innkeeper.

"To sell horses," Ari interjected. "Did you want to buy one?"

"Not today, but I'll ask around for you if you like," the innkeeper replied.

"Yes, thank you."

After their meal, Johann and Ari gathered their horses and continued north.

"He was here!" Johann exclaimed. "We can trace his movements by the inns." New hope lingered in his voice.

One by one, Ari sold his horses. He had taken six with him, and only two remained when he and Johann stopped at an inn for the night. They asked their usual questions.

"Yes," the innkeeper replied, "man named Wilhelm was here and stayed the night."

"Did he say where he was from?" Johann asked.

"If he did, I didn't recognize the village. He's not from our country. That's for sure." The innkeeper clinched his fists and landed them on his hips. "He spoke our language, but he was difficult to understand. And he didn't say much either. Keep to himself he did." Lowering his arms, he asked, "Did you need to get in touch with him?"

"Yes," Ari replied. "We have something for him."

The innkeeper gathered his writing materials. "Write down your name and village. If he returns, I'll give it to him." Ari complied with the request, writing his name rather than Johann's.

The following day, Johann pondered on his father leaving his name and town with the innkeeper. "Papa, that innkeeper gave me an idea."

"What idea?"

"If the keepers of the inns had to record all of their guests who spend the night and their place of origin, then we would know where Wilhelm lives."

"Johann, this is a wonderful idea. You have great talent."

"Maybe, but I am ashamed of myself," Johann confessed.

Ari threw out his hand and stopped his horse and his son's. "Why do you say that, Johann?"

"I have been living a great life in the palace and not seeing how the other subjects live. I have been selfish. I see many

Journey in the Waiting

ways how we can improve the lives of the people here, but I would not have known it if I wasn't looking for Anna."

"Johann, Son, when the Court Physician started his training, did he go out and attend to the patients in need?"

"No." Johann frowned.

"Why not?"

"That would be unwise. He may administer the wrong treatment, and someone could be in a worse condition. Then, no one would trust him. There's so much information to learn before he should treat anyone with certainty and confidence."

"You have just answered your self-imposed guilt."

"What?" Johann replied, wrinkling his forehead.

"Johann, you were in training, too. Now, you're ready to implement what you have learned. You would have widened your world eventually. This search has made that day come sooner."

"Thank you, Papa."

"Geir is a short distance ahead. Let's press on and spend the night at the inn," said Ari.

"Good. I hope the innkeeper knows something about Wilhelm."

The innkeeper had no knowledge of the foreigner. Johann squeezed his eyelids tight, taking in a deep breath. His shoulders slumped forcing the air out of his lungs.

Ari remained calm. "He must have stayed with someone here in Geir. We'll go door-to-door and ask. Let's start with Meta's sister. Minna will want to know about Meta."

Early the next morning, Ari and Johann slowly proceeded to Minna's home. They still had one horse left to sell. Minna saw the two approaching her home. She was excited until she saw their doleful faces. Tomas put his arm around her and patted her arm. When Ari shared everything about Meta, Minna's eyes flooded with tears. When Ari started to talk about the man with the accent, Wilhelm, Minna looked up and smiled. "I know where he stayed!"

D Marie

"Where?" wide-eyed Johann asked. "Please, take us there immediately."

Minna mounted Johann's horse while Johann rode bareback to the place where Wilhelm had stayed, a place outside the village near the coast. An older woman lived there.

Minna knew the woman and vigorously knocked on her door. "Good morning, Minna," the woman greeted her. "How are you today?"

"I'm not well, " Minna replied.

"How may I help?" Tilda asked.

"We're looking for my sister. The man who was staying here knows where she is."

"Please," Tilda began, "everyone, come in."

Ari and Johann related their clues. Tilda occasionally bobbed her head while listening to the information.

Straightening, she shared her knowledge. "I don't know how much help I can give you, but I will try. About two months ago, a man named Matthias came to our village. He was in very poor health. We didn't know it at the time, but he was dying. He stayed at the inn for several days when the innkeeper asked me if I would take him into my home and help take care of him. I talked with the man and found out he wanted to spend his final days by the sea." Tilda stood up and walked over to the window and looked out at the waves beating against the rocky shore.

Turning around, she sighed. "Matthias wasn't from this area. His heavy accent made it difficult to understand him. He mostly sat here by the window and looked out toward the sea. He had a book, but never opened it. He was very depressed." Suddenly, a smile appeared on her face.

"One day, a man named Wilhelm came to visit. Matthias' mood changed for the better. It was a blessing for me, too. Wilhelm took over all of Matthias' physical needs. They were close friends and talked in their language constantly. Wilhelm was also difficult to understand with his accent. I just left them alone and took care of fixing their meals and any other cleaning needs. Wilhelm was a very good Christian friend."

"Why do you think that?" Johann interrupted.

"Because he read a Bible in their language every day."

"You could understand it?" Johan asked.

"No, I cannot understand any of their language, but I can tell by the sections of chapters and verses on the pages that it was a Bible," she replied, folding her arms across her chest and snapping her head in a confident quick nod.

"Another clue, Papa."

"Wilhelm stayed until Matthias passed away. He conducted the funeral and paid for all the expenses," Tilda continued.

"What became of the Bible?" Ari asked.

"Wilhelm took it with him," she replied.

"Did either of them mention where they were from?" Ari asked.

"If they did, I couldn't understand them. They mostly kept to themselves," Tilda recalled. "It was a difficult time for them."

Minna, Ari, and Johann thanked Tilda for her help.

"I wish I could have more information for you," she said. "I will pray for your search every day. Minna, please let me know when you find your sister."

"Thank you for your prayers, Tilda." Minna replied. "When I know they have been found, I'll personally come and share the good news with you."

"Fear not, your loved ones are in good hands," Tilda shared. "Wilhelm will take care of them spiritually, physically, and financially. He's a good man."

Ari and Johann returned to Minna's home, reassuring her that they would find her sister. "The Lord will provide," she said. "Godspeed on your journey."

Johann and Ari gathered their horses and headed for the local inn. The subject of the king came up. Both men listened while the villagers talked.

D Marie

"I hear the town of Christana is prospering. King Albert has given many benefits for the townsfolk. They have a school. The queen and princess help teach the children to read and write," one of the men said, rubbing his beard.

"Why can't we have the same benefit?" a younger man asked.

"You could if you lived near the palace," the older man replied.

"I don't want to move there. This is my home."

Then Johann spoke up, "If a school was started here, how would the teachers be paid?"

"I would gladly pay the crown extra money if we had a school," the younger man said. "I want my children to learn to read and work with numbers."

A low rumble of voices erupted. Other patrons pushed their lower lip upward and dipped their heads in agreement. Ari and Johann smiled, paid their bill, and headed for their rooms.

At first light, Ari and Johann retrieved their horses. "What shall we do with this extra horse, Papa?"

"The Lord will provide a buyer. Let's go to the port to see if the proprietor is interested."

Johann agreed, and they headed south. "Papa, if we hadn't been in the inn when the patrons were talking, we wouldn't have heard their discussion about the school."

"True."

"We need a method to hear the needs and concerns of our people in Christana."

"Let's talk about it on our way to the port. You could call for your counselors to help you when we return home."

"Now, you're thinking like a sovereign." Johann winked at his father.

Increased traffic had compacted the dirt on the path to the seaport. "This trail seems to get wider every time we come here," Ari noticed.

Journey in the Waiting

"Those stumps are freshly cut. The guards must be using these trees for their buildings," Johann added. "I think I hear them now."

Whack, crack, thud. Sounds of activity radiated from the seaport. Tree trunks surrendered their bark to the craftsmen's axes. Large rectangles of wood began to take shape when the sides of the tree trunks were methodically chopped to make support beams for the roofs and walls of the guards' living quarters and work buildings.

The port owner held his bucket in both hands, giving it a quick jerk. Dirty water flew out of the bucket onto the bare dirt. Hearing a horse neigh, he looked up and recognized Ari and Johann. "Good day to you. What news do you have about the finely dressed man?"

"His name is Wilhelm," Johann said. "We discovered where he stayed but don't know where he was from."

Ari's banner caught the eye of the owner, and he walked over to the waving cloth and examined it more closely. "I have seen this cross recently. It's a beautiful design."

Johann and Ari narrowed their eyes on this man. He could almost feel the pressure while he was thinking.

D Marie

"Ah, yes. Now I remember," he said, lifting his pointing finger up in the air. "The baby's blanket had that same cross design on it." Johann leaned toward the man and hung on every word he uttered. "The baby was very fussy, and the woman had to fold the blanket a couple times to quiet her down."

"Papa," Johann said. "A clue!"

"A clue?" the man repeated.

"If you saw the cross and remembered it," Johann began, "others will, too."

"Papa, what should we do?"

"When is the next time for the ship to head south?" Ari asked

"In about nine days," the owner replied.

Ari turned to his son and placed his hand on Johann's arm. "We have time to return to Christana. I will not rest until I find my granddaughter. I'll make the sea journey with my banner."

New hope filled the weary travelers on their way home. At least they had some good news to bring to the worried mother of baby Anna.

Chapter 8

Meta and Anna at Sea

Water lapped at the sides and occasionally went over the rail. The boards creaked from the strain of the wind pushing the sail. The rhythmic motion of the vessel floating on the sea soothed baby Anna and she fell fast asleep. Meta lifted the edge of the blanket and gazed at the baby's face while keeping an eye on the kind man.

Meta reached up and gently rubbed the stitches on her head. Painful to the touch, she lowered her arm. She strained to recall how she had injured her head. Looking at the child, she tried to remember who the baby was. Her thoughts then centered on herself. *Who am I?*

Wilhelm noticed Meta's painful expression. "May I help you?" he asked in her language. His heavy accent obscured Meta's ability to understand. Robbed of her ability to talk, she gave Wilhelm a mournful look that he translated into, "Please help me and the baby."

Anna flung her arms and woke up. Hunger pains turned into cries of need. Meta looked for the ceramic container of milk. Anna had emptied it during her last feeding. Holding the device up, Meta gave Wilhelm another mournful look. Wilhelm scanned the horizon, no ports. He went to confer with the captain and came back with a smile on his face.

"Good news. My port is close. I will get milk from the goat now."

Meta offered a slight smile.

"She may understand some of the words," he muttered. "I'm not sure what she can understand due to her injuries."

Examining the milk bottle, he prayed the goat would be cooperative.

Anna continued to cry after her feeding. Her flailing arms knocked her blanket loose. Meta constantly rocked back and forth to comfort the fussy baby. She watched Wilhelm pace up and down the deck near the rails. He stopped in his tracks. Recognizing the port surroundings, he spun around. "This is where we get off. I'll take you to an inn for food and lodging."

Meta shook her head. Puckering, Wilhelm tried a different method. Using his fingers, he pointed to himself, Meta, and the baby. Then, he made a circular motion with his finger and pointed to the port coming into view. Raising his fingers to his mouth, he pretended to eat. Afterward, he closed his eyes and rested his head on his folded hands.

Meta smiled and nodded.

"She can understand," he mumbled. Turning his head, he watched the deckhands prepare the ship for mooring.

The captain barked the command to lower the anchor. Then he gave the order to launch the rowboat. The other travelers allowed Meta, the baby, and Wilhelm to go ashore first. Only one older man rode with them. The deckhands rowed to shore as quick as possible to be free from the bawling baby.

Wilhelm extended his hand and helped Meta out of the boat. The boat rocked against the dock, causing her to lose her balance. The older gentleman caught her from behind. One more try and she safely disembarked with the baby.

Wilhelm scanned the shops near the shore. He pursed his lips then muttered, "No inn."

The old man heard him. "It's that way," he said, pointing to a nearby street. "I'm going there myself."

Fortunately, the inn had a small reserve of milk. In their rush to get off the ship, they had forgotten about the goat. Anna placed both of her hands on her bottle. Although the end of the bottle felt odd in her mouth, she had adapted to the unfamiliar device and drank the milk. Meta meticulously folded her blanket to the softest level, and Anna finally fell asleep.

Meta had been so distracted taking care of Anna that she hadn't noticed that Wilhelm had disappeared. Fear invaded her eyes. Opening her mouth, Meta tried to make a sound, but nothing came out. The innkeeper tried to console her, but he frightened her and she backed away from him.

The door of the inn opened and Wilhelm walked in. He had retrieved his horse and purchased another one. Meta's eyes pleaded with him. "Don't leave me again." Recognizing her anxious feelings, Wilhelm walked to her side and patted her shoulder. She let out a deep sigh and leaned safely on his side.

The first light of morning streamed through the window and inched its way across the bed where Anna lay. The baby reached out to touched it and cooed. Meta woke up. Her eyes scanned the room, filling her heart with terror. Then, she remembered. *The kind man took me on a trip by water. I'm in a new town.* Meta picked up Anna and affectionately cradled the baby girl in her arms.

"Good morning," a voice behind the door announced followed by a knocking noise.

Meta opened her mouth, but only silence came out. Closing her eyes tightly with gritted teeth, she released her frustration. After laying Anna on the bed, she opened the door. Wilhelm walked in with a fresh bottle of milk and new clothes for Meta and Anna.

Meta's eyes sparkled. She held up the new dress at arms' length being careful not to let it touch her clothes. Dried mud soiled her skirt and blood stained her blouse where it had dripped from her head wound. She smiled at Wilhelm, giving him a nod of appreciation.

Wilhelm's kind face glowed in return. He picked up the baby and the bottle. At the same time, the innkeeper's wife came in with a large pail and towels draped over her shoulder. Steam rose from the water in the bucket. Clutching a bar of soap in her free hand, she pushed Wilhelm out the door.

Wilhelm blinked, trying to keep his eyes open. A good night's sleep had eluded him. With the help of the man from the rowboat, Wilhelm had visited the local shop after their meal and had purchased garments. When he had returned, the rooms were all occupied, so he had piled up the clothing on the table for a soft pillow and had rested there until morning.

"Maybe the baby and I can take a nap together," he muttered. "I wonder who the father is—or *if* she has a father."

Creeeeak went the door. Wilhelm watched the innkeeper's wife come out. She retrieved the satisfied baby and took her into the sleeping room. Wilhelm laid his head down, closed his eyes, and took his well-deserved nap.

Anna flung her arm down and splashed the water. Droplets flung into the air, and she let out a shriek of joy. The other arm came down and splashed the water getting both of the women wet. "I think she's clean, milady," the innkeeper's wife said, and she picked the baby up out of the water.

Meta bundled up her soiled clothing and rinsed out Anna's. The tiny clothing could dry quickly. Glancing around the room, she saw the blanket. Folding it a couple of times around Anna made her snug and warm. Anna yawned, batted her eyes, and drifted off to sleep.

Creeeeak went the door. Wilhelm woke up to see Meta and the child in their new clothes. A grin spread across his face. Retrieving all the bundles, he escorted them to the horses.

"I don't know if you understand, but I'm taking you to a place that will help you get well."

Meta smiled and nodded. *Did she comprehend what I said?* he wondered. *I don't know for sure.*

Chapter 9

Arzt

Wisps of smoke caught Wilhelm's eye. "Almost there," he muttered. The familiar thatched-roof cottage came into view. He pointed to the fork in the road. "This way." Meta followed, pulling the reins to turn her horse toward the town of Artz.

Meta scanned the path and spotted beautiful trees loaded with red fruit hanging from the limbs. Wilhelm, holding both reins in one hand, used his free hand to point his finger. "Kirsche."

Meta scrunched her eyebrows together at the sound of the unfamiliar word.

"I know not the word in your language," Wilhelm replied in his best Christanan vocabulary.

Meta sighed as she shrugged, pulling the corner of her mouth up in a pucker. Looking down, she noticed that her treasured possession was waking up in her arms. Wilhelm also noticed and nodded.

"Almost there," he responded.

Small cottages, arranged in neat rows, appeared lining the path. Soon, the dirt path turned into a stone road leading into the town. Anna vocalized her discomfort at the same moment a large building came into view. Several people milled about in front of the structure, perhaps waiting for someone.

Wilhelm dismounted and held the baby until Meta slid off her horse. Meta held the baby while Wilhelm wrapped the horses' reins around the rail. After examining his clothes, he tried to brush some of the loose dirt off his pants and smoothed his hair back in place. Meta cocked an eyebrow, watching the man fuss over himself. Satisfied with his efforts, Wilhelm motioned for Meta to follow him through the door.

"Good day," Wilhelm acknowledged the first person he saw inside, a physician's assistant. "I just arrived, and I'm looking for a Head Professor, Fritz."

"Follow me, Sir, and I will take you to him," the young woman said.

"Thank you," replied Wilhelm. "I was hoping he would be here today."

"He's with patients at this time but will be finished with his rounds momentarily."

Wilhelm motioned for Meta to follow. The bewildered woman clutched the baby close to her chest. Anna let out a soft cry.

The young woman stopped and walked closer to Meta. Their eyes met. "May I?" she asked, gesturing at the baby, but Meta backed away from the woman.

"She's the reason I need to see Fritz," Wilhelm explained. "Do you have some milk for the baby?"

"Yes! Wait here. I'll get some."

Meta stared at Wilhelm with fearful eyes, not knowing why she was being led around in this building. Her eyes softened when the same woman returned with a new bottle full of milk. Anna's arms swayed back and forth, reaching for the bottle.

When they approached the Head Physician's room, they found the door slightly ajar. "He's back already. You may go in," the young woman said and left.

Fritz looked up and recognized the visitor's face. "Wilhelm, my friend, good to see you. Did the medicine I gave you help your friend?"

"Yes, thank you. It helped to ease his pain."

"How is he now?"

Wilhelm heaved his chest and sighed. "I stayed with him until his passing." Wilhelm's breath became labored. His eyes drooped as grievous memories surfaced.

Fritz laid his hand on Wilhelm's shoulder. "You have my sympathies my friend."

"Thank you, Fritz, and thank you for your help directing me to the new ship route. It made the trip to Christana much quicker."

"Anytime," Fritz replied. The physician curiously glanced over to observe Meta and the baby.

"I have another favor to ask of you," Wilhelm began. "Coming back from my journey, I found this woman near the Christanan seaport. She had a large gash in her head. When anyone tried to communicate with her, she would not speak or write. She has a child. Although I don't think it's hers, she's extremely protective of the baby. When it was time to depart from Christana, she would not leave me. I don't even know her name. That's when I thought of you."

Fritz walked over to Meta and motioned for her to sit down. She complied. Walking behind the chair, he examined the crude but effective stitches. Cupping his hand over his chin, Fritz contemplated the existing symptoms. *Blow to the head, loss of speech, disoriented.*

"Wilhelm, how long can you stay?" Fritz asked.

"I have been absent for a long time, and I need to return to my position."

"Can the woman stay?"

"I was hoping you would help her," Relief softened Wilhelm's face and his tense shoulders relaxed.

"She can stay," Fritz offered. "These cases are rare and our students here will be able to learn from her while we treat her condition. But I cannot guarantee if she will ever be well again."

"What about the child?"

"The child can stay, too. If we separate the two, it could cause further mental damage. We don't want that."

"Thank you, Fritz. I will send money to take care of her expenses. In the meantime, take the horse I'm leaving behind as your first payment."

"We'll set up a private room for her with a baby bed. She should be more comfortable with that arrangement. I suspect she will be distressed when you leave."

"I really don't want to leave her, but I have to get back to work," grieved Wilhelm.

"I understand; we'll take good care of her. Stay here with the woman while I arrange for her room."

"Madam," Wilhelm began, "you will get help."

Meta tilted her head in confusion. Wilhelm pointed to her head and made a painful look. He racked his brain searching for the word for physician or medicine but he drew a blank.

The door opened and the same woman who had led them to Fritz's room walked in. She motioned for everyone to follow. Fritz, Meta, and Wilhelm followed her as she led them down a different hallway and into a room with a bed, rocking chair, and baby bed.

Anna batted her eyes and fought going to sleep. Meta laid the baby on the bed, but she immediately fussed and cried. Spying the rocker in the corner, she sat down to soothe the

Journey in the Waiting

baby. Meta looked up at Wilhelm and smiled. He nodded and left the room.

"Thank you for taking care of them," Wilhelm said to his friend. "I am forever in your debt."

"We do what we can to help the Lord's people. I will send word to you about her progress."

"I'll go get her belongings." Wilhelm paused and looked to the side. "Perhaps you can give them to her later. I don't want her to get upset if she sees me leave again."

"I agree," Fritz replied.

The hospital worker followed Wilhelm to his horse. "These clothes need to be washed."

"I noticed the baby's blanket is very soiled. I will wash it, too. Right now, I'll let them rest," the woman replied.

"Thank you once again. I must be on my way." Wilhelm mounted his horse and turned his head to get one more look at the university. "Lord, help this woman and help me to find her family. Heal her head in Jesus' Name I pray."

Riding out of town took longer than the ride in. Loneliness encroached upon Wilhelm as he missed his traveling companions. "She's married. Where is her family?" he muttered in frustration.

The back and forth motion of the rocking chair comforted Anna and soon she closed her eyes and fell asleep. Meta studied her little bundle. Noting that the baby was taken care of, Meta closed her own tired eyes.

"Ooo, ooo," Anna gurgled, waking Meta.

Meta lovingly watched Anna trying to grasp her finger. *Food,* Meta thought. *The baby needs food, and so do I. Where is that kind man?*

Looking around the room, Meta strained to remember the day's events and where she was. *This must be a place of rest,* she thought. *Horses. We came in on horses. Door. Where is the door we came in? He must be by the door waiting for us.*

Gathering up the baby, blanket, and bottle, Meta headed for the door. Since people entered and left the building at different times, no one paid any attention when Meta left.

One of the horses is missing. I'll go look for him, Meta noted. She untied the horse and tried to get on while holding Anna. A physician-in-training walked by.

"May I help you?" he asked.

Meta nodded, not understanding his words but understanding his offer. The young man gently lifted Anna up. Meta balanced the baby on the saddle with her arm securely wrapped around her. Holding the reins in her free hand, she rode off to look for the kind man.

Chapter 10

Live Life One Day at a Time

Elongated shadows stretched across the yard. The sun slid further behind the trees. Gray smoke rose from the cooking room chimney. Ivar and Ari closed the barn door and headed for the house.

"Papa, I wish Petra and I could be married before we leave, but this feeling in my gut tells me it is not the right time."

"That feeling might be God. If we get out of His timing, we can mess up His plans."

"I'll wait. If I hadn't gone to Herrgott, I would have never met my true love. I can't imagine life without Petra." A revelation of his father's pain of losing his true love hit Ivar and he abruptly stopped. "Papa, your life must have been miserable when Mama died."

Ari inhaled deeply and slowly let it go. He grimaced as the old memories came to the surface. "In the beginning, I was without God and it was miserable. I still miss her, but with God, I can bear it because Jesus gives me His love and strength to endure." They continued to the house in silence.

After dinner, Ari took Angela aside. "The ship will be making its rounds soon. I don't want to be late. Are you sure you will be comfortable here by yourself?"

"I want to stay," replied Angela. "I wouldn't think of leaving during a time like this."

"With Petra and Ivar leaving soon, you will be in this house alone."

"Ari, Jesus is with me all the time. I'm not alone. Besides, Magnus is just around the corner. He and Klaus stay here until sundown."

Seeking comfort, Ari picked up his Bible. Opening it, he ran his fingers across the edges, making the pages turn quickly. Pausing in Romans, one verse caught his attention:

All things work together for good for those who love God and are called according to His purpose.

Looking out the window, Ari poured out his soul. "I don't understand Your purpose, but I truly believe You are working good in this situation."

Angela laid her hand on Ari's shoulder. "Amen. God is faithful, and He loves us. He will show us the way."

"Angela, I'm so happy you came into Magnus' life. I wish my Johanna could see how big our family is growing."

"Somehow, I think she knows. I can't imagine life without Magnus. My parents should be sending word soon about Magnus' letter."

Putting his hand on Angela's shoulder, Ari said, "I think we know what they will say, but it's appropriate to get their approval for your betrothal to Magnus." He grinned. "I certainly approve!"

Angela blushed.

* * *

Klaus' eyes glazed over as he stared at his morning meal and wondered if his brother had found Meta and the baby. Ivar made circles in his porridge with his spoon while Petra did the same thing. Magnus rested his elbow on the table and laid his head in his hand. Ari rested both hands on the table.

Angela scanned the room, noting everyone's behavior. Standing up, she put her hands on her hips. "Is the food that bad? I made it, not Ari."

Ari's frown gave way to a smile and then to a grin. The grin became contagious, and the others caught it.

Journey in the Waiting

"She has you figured out, Papa," said Magnus. "Your horse skills *are* better than your cooking skills."

"Remember the time when you used to cook years ago?" asked Ivar. "Magnus and I would race to eat it so we didn't have to taste it very long."

"That's what was going on?" Ari replied, blinking. "I always thought you were really hungry."

Ari looked across the table. "Ivar, Petra, you two will be leaving soon to start your new journey doing the Lord's work at the castle. If the attack on the palace had not happened, you wouldn't be going there." Ari paused. "God is working in this awful situation. God bless you both for answering the call."

Petra gazed at Ivar, and Ivar squeezed her hand. "Thank you, Papa. I needed to hear that. I'm the one that should be encouraging everybody."

"All Christians need to encourage each other. Otherwise, we can get overwhelmed," Klaus added.

Magnus reached over and gave Klaus a firm pat on the shoulder. "Well said."

Ari cocked his eyebrow. "It does smell better than mine."

"Looks better, too," Ivar chimed in.

"All right, enough. Let's eat." Ari lifted his spoon and savored the taste.

All too soon the meal was over. Ari stood up and gathered his supplies. "Don't forget this!" Angela said holding up the banner.

"I'm so nervous and excited at the same time," Ari replied. "I feel I'm going to find them right away."

"I pray that you do, Ari," replied Angela.

Ari sat down and hung his head. "Angela, what if I don't?"

Angela sat next to him and put her arm around his neck. "We can try to plan for tomorrow, but we can only live life one day at a time."

Tears welled up in Ari's eyes. "Help me, Lord. You provide. You save. You heal. Not my will, but Your will be done." The weight of the uncertainty pulled his head down. "Help me find my granddaughter."

"Ari, I can go with you."

"Thank you, Angela, but I have to do this on my own. It may take many days." Ari picked up his bundles and headed for the door.

"I understand. God bless your journey."

Outside, one by one, everyone said their goodbyes.

Ari mounted his horse and waved to all of them. "This will be the hardest journey I have ever made," he mumbled. His horse plodded down the lane, heading for the palace.

Johann and Tea waited at the gate. The anticipation of using the banner as a clue to find their baby offered new hope. *Will it work?* They wondered. Their eyes followed Ari as he came into view, his banner waving in the wind.

"It's been four weeks since Wilhelm's ship sailed, and two weeks since Benjamin's ship sailed," Johann said. "Maybe he found them. Maybe he's still looking. Oh, how I wished I knew."

Looking steadfast at Ari, Tea pleaded, "Ari find them and bring them home."

Journey in the Waiting

Tea lowered her head on Ari's chest as he wrapped his arms around her. Tears stung his eyes. "I will find them even if I have to knock on every door in every port of call where that ship stopped."

Johann held the horse's reins while his father got in the saddle. "Godspeed, Papa."

"Thank you, I'll take every blessing with me." Lifting his hand in the air, Ari declared, "The Lord provides. Until we meet again."

Johann and Tea watched the horse and rider until they turned the corner and the buildings blocked their view. Tea dabbed her eyes. "What do we do now?"

"Pray and take care of the ones entrusted in our care," Johann said in a non-convincing tone.

"You're right. Mama and I can prepare for teaching. A new group of children will be in our classes this year, Daniel being one of them."

"If you can pry him away from the horses."

"I think he can spare an hour in the morning," Tea added, sporting an amused smile. They walked hand in hand back into the courtyard.

Chapter 11

Taulbe Castle

Neatly packed bundles lay on the table. Taking deep breaths, Petra looked around the rooms one last time. She walked up to her cousin and gave her one last long embrace.

"Petra," Angela said, "we're only two days away. I'll come and visit you."

"You'll have to bring Magnus with you each time," Petra replied.

Angela moved her head backward, scrunching her forehead.

"Magnus is spoiled. His cooking skills are only a little bit better than Ari's."

"You're a funny girl." Angela paused and lowered the corner of her mouth a little. "Petra, we never lived together before. It's been wonderful. I'm going to miss you."

"I'll miss you, too." Petra paused, pursing her lips with a slight smile. "I am excited about what Ivar and I are going to do, sharing the Word with the people at Taulbe Castle. This is a new adventure."

"I bet that castle could use a woman's touch since it hasn't had one in a long time." Locking eyes, they both laughed.

"That's the truth." Petra looked out the window and noticed Ivar coming with their horses. She looked at Angela one more time with tears welling up in her eyes. "Goodbye, Angela. Come soon."

Magnus sat on the church step, waiting for Ivar and Petra. He waited until they reached the steps before he stood up. "This is the first time we will be separated, Ivar. Part of me wishes you well, and part of me wants you to stay."

Ivar dismounted and embraced Magnus, reaffirming that lifelong brotherly bond. "You have Johann right next door, and–" Then, Ivar paused.

"And what?" Magnus asked.

A cute grin spread across Ivar's face. Magnus knew that look. Tilting his head, he waited for the rest of the sentence. "We're identical twins. Just comb your hair my way and look in the mirror. You'll see me!"

Magnus rolled his eyes and shook his head. "Better yet, get those detainees to fix the road between here and the Taulbe Castle. Then it will be a shorter ride. While you're at it, start a village in between so there will be an inn to spend the night." After their round of kidding, silence fell on the two, and they said their last goodbyes.

At the palace, the accompanying female servants and workers placed their belongings in the wagons. Since the path to the castle consisted of rough terrain, they chose to ride a horse instead of sitting in a wagon on the bumpy trail. Eyeing Ivar and Petra at the gate, everyone mounted up. The leader of the garrison of guards took his final headcount before they proceeded to their new home.

Billowing clouds of gray smoke ascended to the sky in the distance, catching the eye of the Head Guard. "Where's that coming from?" he muttered. Quietly, he motioned to the rest of his garrison to look.

Ivar noticed their glances and looked up. *Is that coming from the castle?* he wondered. From that point on, all the guards flanked their charges entrusted into their care.

A fluttering flag greeted the weary travelers when they approached the castle. When the wind blew in the right direction, the flag uncurled to reveal a peaceful looking dove.

Journey in the Waiting

My new home, Petra thought. Looking at Ivar, she smiled. *Our new home.*

A sentry, eyeing the perimeter, spied the approaching caravan and yelled out the discovery. "Reinforcements from Christana are coming. Tell Gunther."

Gunther quickly made his way to the gate. He tried to suppress any visual signs of his enthusiasm but did permit a slight smile to spread across his face. "Open the gates," he commanded.

The Head Guard, still leery of the unexplained smoke, approached the gate first. "Gunther, King Albert bids his good tidings, and all is well."

"All is well here, too. I bid you and your group good tidings. Please come in," replied Gunther.

Satisfied with the response, the Head Guard entered the courtyard looking for the source of the smoke. "Where's the fire? We saw smoke."

"Behind the castle. We have need of more room for our horses. The men are clearing the trees and stumps.

D Marie

"Very well." The Head Guard squinted his eyes and scrutinized the area one more time. Assessing it safe, he allowed his group to enter.

The women rode in first. Gunther's eyes widened as he watched the new guests, more than what he had expected. Ivar accompanied his betrothed while the garrison of guards brought up the rear with the wagons.

Everyone at the castle watched the new inhabitants. Some of the castle guards wondered if they could trade places with the new guards and return home. The detainees marveled at the sight of the women coming to the castle.

"What's their purpose here?" one of the detainees whispered to his friend.

"It's surely a positive sign," another man softly replied.

"Shhh," spoke another detainee. "We'll find out soon enough."

Ivar took Gunther to the side and relayed the information from Christana.

Gunther's eyes sparkled. "The young men that have been sent here are very compliant. They want to do honest work. Truthfully, I believe the older ones want to learn a trade to earn a living and get out of here."

"What about the boys?" Ivar asked.

Gunther turned to look at the young boys in the courtyard. "They want someone to look after them. The ones with no parents look lost."

Ivar scanned the group of youthful looking boys and smiled. "That's why we're here. To save the lost."

"First things first, Ivar. Let's get everyone to their quarters and let them unpack."

Ivar patted Gunther on the back. "Good idea."

Gunther motioned for some of the boys to come forward. "Take the women's belongings to their rooms. They will be there soon." Turning to the group, Gunther greeted them. "Welcome to Taulbe Castle. We will make your stay as comfortable as possible. I'll give you all a tour after you have freshened up from your journey. Then, we will have our evening meal."

The women murmured one to another. Then, Petra spoke up in Herrgott. "When can we start the school for reading?"

One of the boys stopped dead in his tracks. "We get to learn how to read?" His voice caught the attention of the other older detainees.

"Do we get to learn to read, too?" one of the men shouted.

Petra walked closer to the group. Ivar followed by her side. "Who wants to learn to read and write?"

Everyone put their hand up except one man.

Curious, Petra asked, "You don't want to learn?"

The man looked down at the ground, "No, Ma'am. I'm too old to learn."

Petra reached out and lifted his chin. "Are you too old to learn a new trade?"

His eyes widened and the corners of his mouth raised up. "No Ma'am. I want to learn and better myself. I want a family someday. I want to be able to provide for them."

Petra looked up into his gleaming eyes. "You have just found the answer for learning how to read."

The man's eyebrows drew together. "I did?"

"Yes! You said 'I want to learn.' If you want to learn to read, that's half of the process."

The man pursed his mouth. "Hmm." Raising his hand, he said, "I want to learn how to read, too."

"Perfect! As soon as we get settled in, we will start our instructions. We brought supplies with us."

With a respectful curtsy, Petra smiled, put her arm in Ivar's, and returned to her group.

"Why would she want to teach us to read?" one of the detainees asked.

"I don't know, but whatever she knows, I want to know it for myself," confessed another man. A low murmur of voices agreed with him.

Chapter 12

Following the Trail

Sweat trickled down the detainee's forehead. Reaching for his cloth, he glanced out toward the sea. "Here comes the ship," he yelled. The other detainee looked up and waved to the approaching vessel. Turning their eyes toward the Head Guard, the two detainees went back to work on the second new building emerging at the seaport landing.

"Someday, when we have fulfilled our obligations, I want to travel on that ship," the detainee with the scar near his eye said as he nailed a board securely to the wall.

"At least these guards won't hit you over the head with a stick," another detainee said as he retrieved some more nails.

"Yeah, the Hawk Man cured me of disobedience," the man said rubbing his scar. "If I hadn't been under his authority, I wouldn't be learning a decent trade now. Isn't it amazing how things work out?"

"Amazing? That Hawk Man could have gotten us killed. I do agree on one thing. I'm thankful to learn a new trade and to have my past deeds forgiven." The detainee pressed his lips together and lowered his head when Ari walked by.

Ari nodded to the detainees, acknowledging their remarks and kept walking. He approached the guard in charge. "If you see Benjamin, tell him where I'm going. If he has found the baby and the woman, track me down. I'll leave word of my travels in every inn at every port."

"I will," the guard replied.

Rubbing the head of his horse, Ari guided him to the water. "Lord, be with me. I've been in many situations, but this is my first time at sea. Give me strength."

The captain shook his head when he saw his two passengers get closer to his ship. "Another horse. Get the crane ready."

Ari's ears perked up. *Could this be the same captain that Benjamin had?* he wondered. He quickly made his way on board.

"Captain," Ari began, "do you remember a man and his horse that sailed south on the last trip?"

"Aye, the horse was very nervous. The young man was as well. Looking for a woman and her baby he said."

"Do you know where the young man got off your ship?"

Lowering his head, the captain squinted one of his eyes. "And why would you be wanting to know that?"

"The baby is my granddaughter. The woman taking care of her is injured."

"How long ago did the woman and child make their journey?"

"Four weeks."

Grabbing his chin, the captain paused. "I wasn't on duty that trip, neither was the crew. That was our time off. So, I don't know where they disembarked, but I do know where the young man and his horse got off."

"Please, take me there," Ari pleaded.

"With pleasure. It's our first port of call." Ari nodded to the captain and left to comfort his horse in the ship's hold.

For the first time in weeks, Ari relaxed. After currying his horse's back, he sat in the corner and fell asleep.

"Port of call," yelled the first mate.

"Grandpa," yelled the captain into the hold. "We're here."

Ari woke up with a jolt. "Thank you, Captain!" Waiting for the harness to descend into the hold, Ari stayed with his horse to keep him calm. "We're almost there," he said, rubbing both sides of the stallion.

Journey in the Waiting

Once on land, Ari entered the first inn he found. Putting his Herrgott language skills to work, he asked, "Have you seen a young man here two weeks ago? He would be from Christana."

"Yes, I did. I recognized the accent," the innkeeper replied.

"Have you seen a young woman with a child about four weeks ago? She was traveling with a man named, Wilhelm."

"Sir, we have many families staying here. I don't remember those people."

Finding a table, Ari sat down and laid his head on the table while clutching the banner.

"May I get you something to eat?" the innkeeper's wife asked.

"I wish you could get me my granddaughter. I'm trying to find her."

"What does she look like?" the woman asked.

"Golden hair and blue eyes." Raising his hands, he pulled them apart. "She's about this big."

"The cloth you're holding. Where did you get it?"

"My son's betrothed made it."

"I have seen this cross design before on a blanket, the same one. The mother had a head injury of some kind. I helped her and the baby to bathe and put clean clothes on."

Ari stood up. His body towered over the woman, and she stepped backward. "Where are they now?"

"I do not know. They left with no word."

"So close, but I'm on the right path."

Another gentleman in the inn stood up and walked over. "I might know where they went."

Ari's eyes bulged. "Where?"

"Arzt."

"That's what Wilhelm said back in Christana. It means man of medicine, yes?"

"Yes," the man confirmed. "It is also the name of a town a day's ride from here."

"Why do you think they went there?" Ari asked, hanging on every word the man said.

"It's where the University of Medicine is located. I was a passenger on the same ship the woman and her baby were on. We arrived on land in the same rowboat. I saw her head and lack of ability to talk. That's where I would take her."

Another clue, a very good clue. Thank You, Jesus, Ari prayed. "Thank you. If you ever need a horse, I will give you one. My name is Ari, and I live in Christana. My son is the–" Ari paused, thinking about his words, "the minister of church next to the palace of Christana."

"I pray you find your loved ones, Ari. If I ever visit your land, I will come and see you. Godspeed on your journey."

"Did the young man, Benjamin, learn of this information?" Ari asked.

"I never met him," the older man said sadly, shaking his head.

Looking at the woman, Ari waited for her response. "I did not see him in our inn. I'm so sorry." Getting his directions, Ari quickly mounted his horse and headed for Arzt muttering to himself. "Benjamin has a two week start on me. I'll keep looking for him." His thoughts drifted to his granddaughter. *Anna, you have been gone for four weeks already. Pawpaw find you.*

* * *

A month earlier, Meta had looked all afternoon, for the kind man and his noticeable horse, a black horse with four white stocking feet with a white blaze that started at his eyes and went all the way to his nose. Riding around the town, the horse was nowhere to be seen. Anna started to fuss and nightfall started to descend. Remembering the road that she and the kind man had come on, Meta headed for that direction. *Where are the Kirsche trees?* she wondered. *I should see them by now.* She continued on the pathway out of Artz.

Two boys chatting back and forth sauntered out of the woods on to the dusty path in front of Meta. Great terror took over her mind. Backflashes of a stormy night and boys jumping out of the woods appeared before her eyes. She yelled but only a stream of air exited her mouth.

Instincts took over. Several sharp kicks landed into the horse's flanks. The horse neighed loudly in protest and lunged quickly forward, startling the boys and causing them to jump backwards as the horse raced by. Meta rode past twilight and into the night.

"Wah, wah," Anna wailed. A man near the edge of the road saw the horse and rider in the moonlight.

"May I help you?" he asked.

Meta stiffened. *This is not the kind man,* she thought. Meta wanted to ride away, but the path was too dark. *I can't go on.*

"Hilda," the man yelled, "come here."

"What is all this fussing about?" a woman said, opening the door of a cottage. The light inside the house surrounded her body and obscured her face.

"I need your help. This woman seems to be lost."

"Why didn't you say so. Hello, my dear. Let me help you."

Meta clutched the baby even tighter, causing Anna to cry louder, "Wahhh, wahhhh."

"You're scaring her, Hilda. I'll get the reins and bring her closer to the light."

Meta's eyes widened as the man guided her horse toward the humble home.

The woman ran to the house, leaving her alone with the strange man. Carrying a lantern, the woman returned and walked over to Meta. A white cap covered her hair. Rosy cheeks accented her fair complexion. With kind eyes, the woman handed the lantern to her husband and reached out to hold the baby.

Biting her lip, Meta lowered Anna into the waiting arms. She slid off the horse and retrieved the bottle from the horse's pouch. Following the woman holding her crying baby, she submitted to their care and entered the house.

"Sit here, my dear," the woman said.

With pleading eyes, Meta held up the empty bottle.

"Of course, my dear." She kissed the baby's head and handed her back to Meta.

Walking over to the hearth, Hilda lowered her ladle into a kettle of hot water and poured it into the bottle. Poking her head out the doorway, she yelled, "Jakob, we need milk for the baby! Wake up the goat!" Then she poured the dirty water out in the yard.

Hilda walked over to Meta and patted her head, causing her to jerk away. "What's the matter, my dear?"

Meta pointed to her mouth and shook her head. Pointing to her head, she parted her hair and motioned for the woman to look.

"Ouch! I'm so sorry. Don't you worry. I'll take care of you and your baby." Looking at the door, Hilda frowned. "What's taking you so long?"

Jakob walked in with a small bucket of milk. "You didn't say how much, my love." Looking at his bewildered guest, he said, "I'll put your horse in the barn. She will be just fine." Meta gave the couple blank stares.

"Jakob, she has a head injury," Hilda said, pouring the fresh milk in the clean bottle. "We need to take care of her. She can't talk either."

"Does she understand us?" Jakob asked.

"I don't know. You stay with her. I'll fix up the bed in the spare room."

Anna opened her eyes in between her cries. Meta placed the bottle near her mouth. Anna reached up for the bottle and quickly drained it dry. Hilda returned to the cooking room. She stopped and watched the baby in the arms of the injured woman. *What a lovely sight,* she thought and sighed. *We have never had a baby in this home. Thank You, Jesus, for sending them to us. We'll take good care of them.*

"Ahem," Hilda loudly vocalized, clearing her throat and mind at the same time.

Journey in the Waiting

Meta looked at the woman and noticed cloths for changing the baby dangling from her hands. Meta met her eyes and offered a grateful look. Standing up, Meta nodded and followed Hilda into the spare room.

Jakob remained in the cooking room, contemplating his new house guests. "That woman looks out of place," he muttered. "Where did she come from?"

Closing the door behind her, Hilda joined her husband. "They're resting now. What should we do, Jakob?"

"I don't think she's from around here."

"She may not be a local citizen, but she is a Christian."

"What makes you say that?" Jakob asked. "She hasn't uttered a word."

"The baby's blanket, Jakob. It has a beautiful stitched cross on it. She folded it just right and the fussy baby went right to sleep. Maybe she likes the smell of it." Hilda paused, casting her eyes downward. "Jakob, can we let them stay?" *Forever,* she said quietly to herself.

Jakob studied his wife's face. Pressing his lips together, he took a deep breath. "Hilda, the good Lord has not blessed us with a child. But He has guided this woman and baby to our home. The Good Book says in Matthew about feeding Jesus when He was hungry, and giving drink when He was thirsty, and when He was a stranger, He was invited in and clothed. The disciples questioned Jesus about those words, and He told them, 'When you did for the least of my brothers and sisters you did it to Me.' I believe this is what He was talking about."

Jakob picked up his wife's hand with both of his hands. "Yes, we will take care of them. But we must try to find out where they live."

"What if we tie her horse to the tree by the lane? Maybe someone will recognize it."

"Great idea."

"What if no one does, then what?" Hilda asked looking dolefully in her husband's eyes.

"We'll pray for an answer," Jakob said with a wink and his warm smile. "Right now, it's time for our evening prayers. It will take a little longer tonight since we have two more to pray for."

* * *

"Benjamin, where are you?" Ari muttered. "Lord, show me a sign." Thunder rolled in the distant sky.

"Rain?" Ari stopped his horse and looked up. "Lord, I don't need rain right now. Please let me have good weather. Otherwise, I won't see the path I should take." His eyes drifted downward. The clouds latched together and choked the last rays of the evening sky. Ari looked up again. "It rained the night Meta fled the palace, and she got lost."

Ari exhaled deeply and gently pressed his legs into his horse's flanks. "Tsk tsk," he commanded, and the horse moved forward. Jerking the reins back, he quickly hollered, "Whoa! Lord, thank You! A sign! The night Meta rode away, it rained. She went right at the fork in the road. Help me find the right path."

Pulling his coat tight around his neck, Ari tried to keep the rain from soaking his shirt. "I need to stop and spend the night some place—hopefully, not in the rain."

A faint light appeared in the distance, and then another light appeared. "A settlement! I hope they have an inn." His eyes scanned the buildings. He couldn't see an inn, just small cottages. One of the homes had a barn with a glow illuminating the windows.

"Hello," Ari yelled. But the cracking thunder drowned out his voice. "Hello," he hollered again, guiding his horse closer to the barn.

The light in the window bobbed up and down. It shown brighter when an elderly man stood in the doorway, holding his lantern. "May I help you? Please come inside out of the rain."

Journey in the Waiting

The old man listened to the stranger's story while watching water drip from Ari's face. He offered his hand in friendship. "Good to meet you, Ari. I am Kai. Your Herrgott words are not so good. The same as a young man here many days ago."

Ari's eyes bulged. "Brown hair, on a brown horse?"

"That's about half of the people I see, but he did talk about a woman named Meta."

"That's him! Which way did he go?" Ari asked.

"Not the way to Arzt. He took the wide path. You passed the narrower path to go to Arzt. Only a person familiar with this area would know the difference."

Ari dropped his head. The elderly man put his weather-beaten hand on his shoulder. "Young man, spend the night here in my barn. I will call you for food in the morning."

Ari nodded.

Raising his pitchfork, the elderly man tossed clean straw in a corner while Ari removed the saddle from his horse. With his hand held out, Ari offered the man payment.

The old man looked at the hand and smiled. "Maybe you may want to try my cooking before you pay."

Ari's chest moved in and out as he chuckled. *We have the same talent for cooking,* he mused.

Sunlight inched across the floor until it reached Ari's eyes and woke him up. Startled, he swung his arms around. "Where am I?" A loud neigh followed. Rubbing his neck, Ari walked to his horse and rubbed his long forehead and sleek sides. "Eat up, boy, we have another long ride today."

The sound of a wooden spoon striking a pan reached his ears. The familiar aroma of porridge floated in the air, welcoming Ari into the cottage. Steam rose from the bowls resting on the table. Looking around the cottage, Ari figured out why he had slept in the barn. The cottage only had one large room.

Looking across the table, the old man took pity on Ari. "Young man, I will take you to the correct path. It's not far."

D Marie

"Thank you, I'm eager to get going," Ari replied and he set some coins on the table.

The old man walked by and picked up the payment and tucked it away into his pocket. "Let's saddle up."

Twenty minutes later, they approached the fork in the path. The elderly man rubbed his chin. "Just as I thought."

Ari tilted his head toward Kai. "What is it?"

"The sign fell down." Getting off his horse, the man picked up a worn plank and shoved its stake back in the ground. "The wind probably knocked it down. The locals know the road, and don't stop to fix the sign."

Four letters and an arrow gave Ari the biggest clue he needed.

A huge smile spread across his face, and his eyes beamed. "It says Arzt! Thank you, Kai, and thank You, Lord. I can find Meta and Anna and take them home." Ari leaned toward the aged man. "If you see Benjamin again, tell him what happened. If the woman and child are in Arzt, I'll take them back to Christana. Goodbye, my friend." Ari pressed his heels into his horse and rode away.

Chapter 13

River Work

Pain throbbed in the detainee's hand. "Ow!" He pulled his hand away from the stuck wagon wheel and gaped at his new blister. His thumb slid over the palm of his other hand where calluses had replaced his old blisters.

"Break time's over," his friend scolded. "Wrap this rag around your hand and help me turn the wheel."

"Do you think we have enough stones?" the man with the blister asked.

"I hope so. I want to learn how to mortar them together. I can earn money doing this."

"It's working," a guard murmured as he walked by.

His fellow guard nodded. "Maybe these men will be ready to join our city again once the bridge is completed."

"I agree," came a distinctive voice from behind them.

The guards stiffened. "Your Majesty," one of the guards greeted and bowed.

King Stefan raised his hand and shook his head. "Fear not. We need positive watchmen for our detainees while they rehabilitate back into our society. I don't want them mistreated. *That* would lead to resentment."

Lowering their heads, the guards acknowledged the king's words.

The rumbling of the water increased in volume as they approached the edge of the river. King Stefan closed his eyes, imagining the pain his son had caused when he was alive. Opening his eyes, he saw the banner with the dove mounted on the castle rampart as it fluttered in the wind. Taking a deep breath, he released the negative feelings and received the comfort of new opportunities, beginning with the building of the bridge.

Surveying the landing, Stefan observed piles of cut stones stacked in several rows, waiting for their final resting place, and cut timber laying behind the stones. He noticed sweat pouring down the faces of the men at the river's edge while they kept digging deeper into the dirt. An adolescent boy appeared and dipped his bucket in the river. He walked from man to man, offering them cool water from his ladle.

A man approached the visiting group and bowed. "Your Majesty, we have the plans ready for your inspection."

"Thank you, Head Architect. I am pleased with your work," King Stefan replied. "How are we on supplies? I want to get the foundations in before winter."

"We're right on schedule. With all of these men, we were able to prepare the stones faster than expected. We'll start transporting some of them to the opposite side soon."

Stefan nodded and sought after the guards by the river. "I want to go to the castle. Prepare the rowboat."

The Head Guard's eyes widened slightly. "Yes, Sire." *Can the king swim? I'll go with him,* he thought.

Strands of silver hair flowed in the wind. Reflecting on the last time he was in a boat, Stefan regally sat in the bow, watching the detainees on shore work with the stone masons. Laying a straight edge on the stone, the stone mason demonstrated how to chisel off the imperfections. "Soon these detainees will have a marketable trade," he murmured. A slight smile of inward satisfaction resided on his face.

Fighting the current of the Vogel, the oarsmen grunted as they inched their way across the river. "Toss your rope," a stern voice hollered from the opposite shore, and he pulled the rowboat next to the dock. The man bowed. "Your Majesty, allow me to help you out."

Stepping out of the boat, Stefan offered his hand. "Thank you, young man. Now, escort me to the castle."

Flap, flap, flap. The crisp sound of the flag captured Stefan's attention. A tightness squeezed his chest.

I've not been here since my son moved in. I've made so many mistakes. Looking up, he silently prayed, *Jesus, this time I pray to You first. Help me make good decisions about the future of Herrgott for Your glory and for Your people. Show me Your ways.*

Stefan sighed, his eyes drooping, and followed the guard up the stairs, huffing and puffing along the way. The two guards in front heard their king's struggle to breathe. Their eyes met and they proceeded at a slower pace.

Gunther waited for the group at the top of the stone stairs. "Good morning, Your Majesty." King Stefan raised his head and glared at Gunther. Gunther immediately corrected himself. "Good morning, Stefan."

Stefan's face softened. "Good morning, Gunther. I'm pleased to see the progress of the bridge. Your detainees seem to have acclimated to their new training."

"They have been most cooperative, needing very little discipline."

An eyebrow cocked as Stefan waited for a more detailed explanation.

Gunther gulped and continued, "The detainees working in the castle want to be working on the bridge, too. There have been grumblings and complaints, but it has stopped."

Stefan's brow furrowed in curiosity.

"The groups will switch roles when it's time to construct the wooden frame for the arch that goes over the river."

"Ah, good compromise, Gunther." Looking at the river bank, Stefan asked, "When will the frame be started?"

"As soon as the stones reach a certain height. We will start from both sides of the river. The weather will be cold and the river traffic will be slow during that time."

"What happens when the river freezes?"

Gunther smiled. "That's when we can join the two sides with braces and make the completed arch. When it warms up, the masons can lay the stones over the wooden structure."

"Can the vessels sail under the wooden structure?" Stefan asked.

Gunther frowned. "Not sure about that. The completed arch will be high, but the wooden braces may not permit passage if the vessels have a tall mast. That's why we are working on it all the time. The Head Architect keeps us informed of the progress."

"Good." Stefan took one last look at the river. "Let's go inside. How is Ivar doing?"

"He's a born leader. I'm so glad he's here. Ivar sees things I do not, and he shares his thoughts with me with the upmost consideration to my position. He really cares for these men and wants them to succeed."

"And the women? How are they adjusting?"

"Let's put it this way," Gunther chuckled a little. "This man's castle has changed a little."

Again, Stefan scrunched his eyebrows together.

Gunther continued, "They're like mother hens to these men. It's like they give the detainees the maternal love they may not have had for a while—maybe never had at all."

"What do they do?"

"The women run the school. If their students slouch, they gently nudge them back in line. Sometimes, I think their students do it on purpose to get extra attention." Gunther paused and winked. "I would."

Stefan let go of a hearty laugh and placed his hand on Gunther's shoulder. "Well done."

Passing the door into the courtyard, Stefan's eyes slowly scanned the interior. He imagined his son looking out of a window and waving at him. Stefan took a deep breath and sighed. *I love you, Son.*

A nearby horse neighed, interrupting Stefan's vision. He turned around and saw Ivar leading a horse by its reins.

"Good morning, King Stefan," Ivar said, remembering how to address royalty in public.

"Good morning, Ivar. It's good to see you. How do you like working with the Edelross horses?"

"Your Majesty, you have given me such an honor. I get to share the Gospel with the people here, and I get to work with horses again." Ivar's eyes sparkled. "Your horses are magnificent. I wish our citizens could see them, too."

"Hmm," Stefan muttered as he stroked his short, but growing, beard. "That's an interesting idea. We must meet sometime and discuss more of your ideas, Ivar."

"I'm at your service, Your Majesty." Ivar bowed his head to the sovereign.

"If you need anything, let me know," Stefan said, walking away.

"There is one thing," Ivar said. Stefan stopped and turned around. "I would like to build a church next to the castle. We don't have much ground inside the courtyard for the foundation."

A smile spread across Stefan's face while thinking about the request. "A church is an excellent idea. This could be the first paying job for our 'future former detainees' after they complete the bridge."

Ivar tried to suppress his enthusiasm and nodded to the king.

Gunther escorted Stefan through the castle, and Ivar continued to work with his beautiful white stallion. Catching Ivar's eye, Petra waved from the balcony. *The Lord is good, all the time,* he thought. Then, he thought about his missing niece, baby Anna. *Even if we don't understand His ways.*

Chapter 14

The Long Summer

Another tear fell and trickled down her cheek. Tea gazed out of the window facing the woods. "Where are you, my little one?" She spoke so softly that only the breeze flowing into the room could hear. Approaching footsteps alerted Tea and she quickly dabbed her eyes.

Not fooling Johann, he held his wife and comforted her. "They'll find her, Tea. I know it. Deep in my heart, I know it."

"You have deep faith, Johann. I do too, but I want my baby back." Her lips trembled and tears rolled down her face again.

"When this is over—and it will be over someday—we will see God's plan and what He wanted to do. In the meantime, and I know this is hard—" Johann paused and lifted Tea's chin up to look into her eyes "—let's sing praise songs to God. If praise songs can bring down the walls of Jericho and build up the Israelites' faith, it can help us, too."

"Pick out a Psalm, Johann. We can read it together."

Johann hastened to pick up the Bible. His father had lent the family Bible to him before he left. He moaned inwardly as he held the Bible, remembering the times he had read this Book growing up on the family farm. He thumbed through the pages, looking for his favorite chapters. One chapter stood out bolder and caught his eye.

"The 100th chapter of Psalms says to *'give God thanks and praise his Name. For the Lord is good and His love endures forever.'*" Johann stopped and looked at the scripture again.

D Marie

"Tea, that's what we need to do: thank Him and praise His name. He didn't cause our daughter to be missing. We decided to get her out of town. Our faith will increase the more we think positively by thanking the Lord and praising Him."

Tea breathed deeply in and out. "It's difficult, Johann. I hoped this would be a short separation. We have no guarantee when they will be found, but the Lord knows. So, I will put my focus on that." She lowered her head and prayed, "Thank You, Lord, for what You are doing, and I praise You while You're doing it. I know You love us. In Your Name, I pray, Jesus. Amen."

"Amen," Johann added.

"Johann, Let's go see Reverend Lars."

"Is there a special reason for the visit?" Johann asked.

"Yes, the remaining detainees here need spiritual guidance, and Lars is the one to help them. Magnus is busy with his church duties. Lars has more time."

"Good idea."

"And…" Tea paused. "If they want to learn to read, I will teach them."

"Are you sure about that?"

"It's been on my heart. It's time I listened to the call."

"Well Ma'am, let's go find Lars." Johann and Tea walked to the church with lighter hearts while focusing on the needs of others rather than on their own.

* * *

Taking slow steps, King Albert headed for the horse pasture. Memories of the attack invaded his mind every time he went there. Passing the gate, his jaw dropped. The remaining detainees stopped their work and bowed most respectfully. Then, they returned to their duties. The pasture never looked so clean. The stable for the mares had been recently painted. The corral had new boards. Entering the stable for the guards' horses, the inside floors had been swept and washed.

The Head Guard approached Albert. "Good morning, Sire. The detainees have been very busy. We don't have enough work for them to do."

"What do you suggest?" Albert asked.

"I have heard that the seaport where our guards have been assigned needs more helpers."

Albert pursed his lips while thinking about the suggestion. "How well do you trust these men?"

"I cannot guarantee their behavior, but they are cooperative and want to be productive. Reverend Lars has had an impact on their lives."

"How so?"

"These men had very little knowledge of God and the Bible. They are eager to learn, Sire."

Albert paused to consider the report.

"Perhaps sending a few men at a time and rotating them with another group would be a good start," the Head Guard added.

"Good suggestion. I'll investigate the needs of the port. Prepare a horse for me and four guards."

The man bowed as Albert left.

"Maria," Albert called, entering the library.

She laid her book down and looked up. "Yes, Albert."

"I'm going to the seaport. I want to see what is going on there." Maria's eyes widened. "Don't worry. I'm taking guards with me."

"Will you be back before dark?"

"Yes, and sooner if I can go right now," he said with an amused grin.

Maria chuckled and winked. "You may go."

"See you tonight."

The horses neighed loudly, stomping the ground with their hoofs. Perhaps they sensed they were getting a chance to get out of the confined area of the palace pasture. The side gate opened, allowing the group to leave.

It's been too long since I have ridden in this direction. I need to get out more, Albert thought. Being more familiar with the area, the Head Guard pointed to the arrow rock. Albert immediately knew its significance to turn here.

The owner of the small inn on the way to the port watched the colorful group of riders go by. "Is that King Albert?" he asked his wife.

"It's him or someone else important," she replied.

"It might not be the king. He's not wearing a crown."

"Maybe it's uncomfortable to ride with it on."

"Good point, wife. That's why I don't wear mine. It's too uncomfortable," the innkeeper teased.

His wife turned her back and rolled her eyes. "Yes, Your Majesty. It's time to get back to work, Your Majesty."

Albert's group disappeared over the rise in the path, unaware of the entertainment they had just provided. The fragrance of the salty sea that floated in the air greeted their noses when they passed the top of the path. They saw several buildings near the sea. The oldest buildings had wooden crates and barrels stacked by their sides. The guards' barrack stood a short walk away.

One of the guards noticed the entourage coming and alerted the others. They stood at attention when the king came closer.

"Your Majesty," the workers said.

"Carry on," Albert replied and dismounted.

Albert walked around the environment, noticing the dimensions and workmanship of the operation. He turned to observe their current building, which they had just started.

"How does it go here?" Albert asked.

One of the guards made a slight pucker with his mouth. He immediately noticed the king staring at him and lowered his head.

"Young man, do you wish to say something?" Albert asked.

The young man gulped. "Sire, pardon me."

"Go on."

"The walls are difficult to raise with so few of us. We're willing to do the work, but we need more manpower." He lowered his head.

"If you could have more manpower, how much would you need?"

The workers huddled together. Low unintelligible murmurs could be heard. "Four or more men would be appreciated," the young guard replied.

"If they were detainees, would you have room for them?" Albert asked.

"We could house four more easily. That would make a total of six detainees," the young guard said. The other guards nodded in agreement.

"Is tomorrow soon enough?"

"Yes," they all said.

"I'll see to it. Good work, men." Albert summoned his escorts and returned home.

Chapter 15

Ari's Agony

Clammy sweat covered the palms of his hands, and he wiped them on his pants again. Occasionally, streams of sunlight forced its way in between the tall trees and struck his eyes stingingly. Ari squinted again. Raising his hand to his forehead, he tried to block the sun's rays. "Arzt has to be close. I'm seeing more and more cottages," he murmured.

The sight of the Kirsche trees brought back warm memories when Johann had mispronounced the Herrgott word and said church tree instead of cherry tree. The path widened into a road paved with cobblestones. Ari reached out and patted his horse's neck. "Remember the smooth stones you had to walk on during your training days back on the farm? Here they are, my friend."

Using his best Herrgott words, Ari asked a man walking across the road, "Which way to the school?"

The man's eyebrows scrunched. Ari tried again, this time holding his arm as if in pain. "Physician? School? Ow, ow!"

The man smiled and nodded, pointing to the street to the right. He raised two fingers. "Two streets."

Ari nodded and rode in that direction. A smile spread across his face when he found the large building. "This reminds me of the twins' school of ministry." His heart raced, thinking this might be the end of his journey. He tied his horse to the rail and entered the building while clutching his banner. "I am looking for a woman and child. A man named Wilhelm brought them here."

The woman gave him a puzzled look, being unable to understand this stranger's words. Ari talked slower and used sign language. He rocked his arms back and forth and said, "Wah, wah, wah." Then he raised his hand pointing to his head and said, "Ow."

The woman's eyes bulged at the sight of the banner and her jaw dropped. Ari interpreted her reaction and his heart pounded. He knew he had made his intentions known, but the woman's reactions made his stomach churn. She shoved her hands downward and said, "Stay, wait."

Ari watched her run down the hallway. When she turned the corner, he kept his eyes glued to the empty corridor. Finally, a man in a white coat appeared with the woman by his side.

"Hello, my name is Fritz. I am the Head Physician here."

Ari sighed. "You can speak my language. I am Ari of Christana. Have you seen a woman and a baby recently here?"

"We see many people here. Who are you looking for?"

"A baby and a woman caring for her. The woman was injured when she fell from her horse. She was seen with a gentleman, Wilhelm. Maybe he brought her here."

The physician studied Ari's face. "How do you know these people?"

Ari, annoyed at the line of questions, raised his voice, "The baby is Anna, my granddaughter. The woman is Meta, my friend's wife. Are they here?"

"Follow me please," Fritz said. He guided Ari to his office. "Please sit down."

Confusion covered Ari's thoughts. He wanted to lash out, but he held his tongue.

"Ari," Fritz began, "a friend of mine brought the woman and child here. He hoped that we could help her."

"What's wrong with her?" Ari interrupted.

"She seemed dazed as if she didn't know who she was, and she couldn't speak."

"Can you help her?" Ari's voice cracked.

"We won't be able to help her."

"Maybe when she sees me—"

Fritz held up his hand. "Ari," Fritz paused, "she's gone."

Ari jumped out of his chair and glared at the physician. "What do you mean she's gone? Who took her? Where's my granddaughter?"

Fritz walked closer to Ari and helped him back to his chair. "We don't know. My friend left her here and left her horse as payment for treatment. Later, when we came back to her room, she and the baby were gone. Her horse was gone, too."

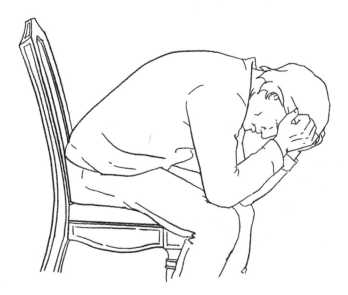

Ari hung his head while hope spilled on the floor. "Anna, where are you?" Looking up, he asked, "Is it possible that your friend came back and took her away?"

"It is possible, but Wilhelm would have informed us if he had."

"Wilhelm, who is he?"

"He's the Rector at the University of Ministry in Herrgott. It's near the royal palace. Have you heard of it?"

Ari's eyes widened. "I, I–" A momentary scene of the day that his twin sons graduated from that university flashed before

Ari's eyes, and he blinked. "What is the quickest way to get there?"

"Did you come down the path where the Kirsche trees grow?"

"Yes, I did."

"Go back the same way and turn south where it meets the next road."

Bending his head down, Ari took several deep breaths. He closed his eyes to focus on his next mission. That's when he heard a still small voice deep inside his spirit. "I am with you always." Immediately, Ari raised his head and looked around the room. Fritz gave no indication that he had heard it. Then, Ari smiled. "Thank you, Sir. If Meta returns, send word to my son, Ivar, he works in the castle by the two rivers."

"I have heard of this place," Fritz began. "The Vogel River is not far after you make the turn in the path. You could get to the river by nightfall. There's an inn there."

"Thank you, Fritz."

"Godspeed on your journey, Ari." Ari nodded and headed for his horse.

The afternoon sun shone on Ari's face and gave him comfort. It seemed to sustain its light to allow enough time to find the river's edge. The water lapped at the edges of the bank, creating a soothing sound. A boat had docked for the night at the long dock extending out into the river. The sun quickly extinguished its light as Ari walked into the inn. Sitting down in a chair, he lowered his head, almost falling asleep.

The innkeeper tightened his apron when he approached his guest. "Good evening, Sir, how may I help you?"

"I'm looking for a woman with a baby. She may be by herself or traveling with a gentleman. Have you seen them?"

The innkeeper paused, trying to decipher Ari's question and answered with a few chosen words. "Woman, baby, here?"

"Yes." Ari's tired eyes narrowed in on the innkeeper, waiting to hear his response.

Looking down, the innkeeper rubbed his chin. He went into deep thought and shook his head. "No, no baby. You want food?"

Ari's shoulders drooped. "I do not want food. I am tired and need a room."

The innkeeper picked up a few words that he understood: tired and room. "A room then. Follow me." He motioned for Ari to follow. Afterward, he gave orders to his son to take care of the new horse outside.

"Thank you," Ari mumbled and crashed onto the narrow bed. He fell asleep on the instant.

The innkeeper stared at the door and muttered, "Is he all right? He's slept passed the morning meal. Maybe I better knock."

A few moments later, the door opened. Ari yawned. He made his way to the tables and chairs. "Good morning," he said.

"Good afternoon," the innkeeper replied.

"I slept that long?"

The innkeeper smiled and shrugged." Food, Sir?"

"Yes, please."

Steam carried the aroma of the stew up to Ari's nose. Inhaling the aroma planted a smile on his face. Even the vegetables floating in the broth looked especially tasty. "Very good food."

The innkeeper smiled and scratched his head. *Not too many of my guests compliment my cooking. What did I do different today?* Seeing his son nearby, the innkeeper motioned for him to get Ari's horse ready.

"What do I owe you?" Ari asked.

"You are a kind man. The room, one coin." Then the innkeeper patted his chest. "The food, I pay."

"Thank you," Ari replied. "Have you seen a young man from Christana? His name is Benjamin."

Studying the words, he heard Benjamin. "Yes, Benjamin here last week," replied the innkeeper.

"Do you know where he went?" Ari asked.

"To the river trail. Benjamin, very sad. Didn't talk much."

Ari understood and nodded.

Ari looked at his pouch of coins and took out another one. Taking the hand of the innkeeper's son, he placed the coin there. "Thank you for taking care of my horse."

The boy's eyes widened, staring at the coin in his hand. "Thank you, Sir. Please come back."

With a wave of his arm, Ari headed for the confluence of the Vogel and Herrgott Rivers. *I wonder what that castle looks like on the inside.* More serious thoughts flooded Ari's mind. *Benjamin, are you still there?*

Rushing water interrupted Ari's thoughts. Turning the bend, he could see several men digging near the river bank. Stacks of stones and timber waited on both sides of the river. Grunts and groans of men, pulling long saws through the logs making cut boards, wafted through the air. One of the guards on the opposite side of the waterway motioned for the guard near the castle to be aware of the rider on horseback coming his way.

Sensing the tight security, Ari identified himself. "I'm Ari of Christana, father of Ivar."

The nearby guard nodded to Ari when he rode by. The castle hill rose quickly from the river's edge. Ari dismounted and climbed the stairs pulling his horse's reins all the way to the top and into the gate.

"Father!" a familiar voice rang out.

"Ivar!"

Ivar raced to his father's side, wrapping his arms around him. Then, Ivar stepped backward and reality set in. His father was alone. "What news do you have?"

"You may know of the man that found Meta and Anna. His name is Wilhelm."

"Wilhelm? The only Wilhelm I know is in Herrgott at my university."

"It was him," Ari replied watching his son's reaction.

Journey in the Waiting

"Father, he is a very honorable man. He would do anything in his power to help Meta and Anna."

"He did. He took them to the University in Arzt to get Meta help, but—" Ari paused and deeply sighed.

"But what?"

"Meta and Anna disappeared. They don't know where she went. Her horse disappeared, too."

Ivar backed up to the wall, his face turning pale. "She rode away alone?"

"No one knows. I'm on my way to Herrgott to look Wilhelm up."

"I'll go with you."

"I appreciate the company, but you are needed here."

"At least take a guard with you that knows the path," Ivar pleaded.

"I will. Did Benjamin get here?"

Ivar lowered his eyes. "Yes, he did. Papa, it was pitiful. He's in so much pain."

"Is he here now?" Ari asked.

"No, I convinced him that Josef needs him. He finally agreed and went home."

Ari heaved his chest and slowly expelled the air. "Don't send any word about my findings until I return from Herrgott. Maybe Wilhelm can help us."

"I pray he does. Let's go find Petra. She probably knows you're here by now."

Chapter 16

Home

One drop fell and then another. The guards pulled their collars tight around their necks in a vain attempt to keep dry. Occasionally, they glanced back at the rider bringing up the rear. They all felt sorry for him, but Benjamin felt nothing except the pain in his heart.

Benjamin wanted to return home alone, but Ivar had other plans. Under the guise that it was time to rotate a group of guards, Ivar dispatched six men to accompany their charge and take care of his needs during the journey back home. The woods offered no inns for sleeping or food.

After two days of travel, outlying cottages came into view, indicating that Christana was nearby. Benjamin stared at the ground for most of the journey home. The bustle of activity near the town square caused him to look up.

"What am I going to tell Josef?" Benjamin's chest heaved in and out. His stomach churned.

"Papa!" a young voice rang out through the opened gate. Josef ran to his father, leaving Daniel by the gate.

Benjamin slid to the ground, grabbed his son into his arms, and lifted him up off his feet. "Oh Josef, I have missed you so much."

"I've missed you, Papa. Where's Mama?"

The question that Benjamin had no answer for came crashing in on his head. *What do I say, Lord?*

A silent voice rang in his head, and Benjamin share it. "Mama is still with Baby Anna."

"I wish she was here, but Anna needs her more." Josef looked into his father's eyes. "Can you stay with me while we wait for them?"

Benjamin hugged his son even closer if that was possible. "Yes, Son."

"Good. Let me show you what I have." Josef grabbed his father's hand and led him to the horse gate. Josef's eyes sparkled as he looked across the field. "See that horse over there? He's mine!" Josef ran all the way to the corral and called for his friend. He looked around for Daniel but didn't see him.

The horse trudged closer to the rail when he saw a carrot in the boy's open hand. He had less bounce to his step, and the gray hair around his eyes and muzzle stood out on the dark brown coat that did not have the typical sleek look anymore. Raising his upper lip, the once mighty steed nibbled on the tasty treat.

Benjamin covered his mouth, stifling his grin. Clearing his throat, he reached out to pat the horse. "Fine looking horse you have here."

"The guards said if I promise to ride and groom him, he's mine."

Tilting his head sideways, Benjamin eyeballed the horse. "The guards have chosen well. This fine fella needs a boy like you to keep him active."

"Can I keep him? The guards said I have to ask you."

"Only if you promise me one thing."

"What's that, Papa?"

"You will always ask me before you ride and stay in the pasture area unless we ride together outside the walls."

Josef leaned into his father and hugged him. "I promise."

"What's his name?"

"Papa."

"Yes, Son. What is the horse's name?"

"I named him, Papa."

"Why did you pick that name?"

"I missed you and wanted to call someone Papa while you were gone."

Benjamin lowered himself and gather Josef in his arms. "I will not leave you again."

Johann and Tea came running to the pasture. "Benjamin!" Johann yelled.

Standing up, Benjamin patted his son on the shoulder. "I need to talk to Johann. I'll be back in a few minutes.

"All right, Papa. I'll be here with–," Josef looked up then his eyes glimmered. "Spirit! It reminds me of the Holy Spirit."

"Good name, Josef. You choose well." Benjamin patted his son again and turned his eyes toward baby Anna's parents.

The walk to the gate was the worst part of his journey. *Lord, I need Your help again. What do I tell them about their daughter?*

Tea reached out and touched Benjamin's cheek. "Did you find them?"

Looking down, Benjamin struggled to hold back the tears. His chin quivered. "No. No one recalled seeing them."

Tea picked up Benjamin's hands in hers. "Benjamin, Ari left on the next ship with a very important clue."

Raising his head, Benjamin asked with pleading eyes. "What is it?"

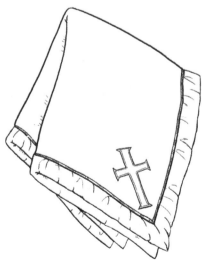

"The port master remembered the cross on Anna's blanket when he saw Father's banner. He left with his banner to look for them," Johann said.

"This is promising, but how can you be so calm?"

"Psalms 100," Tea replied. "We're using the method the Lord requires, thanking Him and praising Him. Believe me it's not easy, but it's better than the overwhelming grief we were carrying all the time."

"Johann? Does it help you, too?" Benjamin asked.

"Absolutely. Like Tea said, it's not easy, but I have to trust His Word and promises."

"I will try, too. If not for me, then for my son."

"Let's go see how his horse is doing. He's been wanting to get up in the saddle."

A loud neigh emitted from the stable window at the end of the pasture. Benjamin looked toward that direction. "The Edelross mares are still here!"

"Yes, and they need training. Interested?" Johann asked.

"Me?"

"Not me," Tea grinned. "I'll be busy teaching children to read."

"What kind of training? I don't know the Edelross method."

"What about the course your brother Klaus is using?" Johann suggested. "I trained many horses on that course."

"The farm, yes, it's a good start." Looking at his son, Benjamin yelled, "Saddle up Spirit, Josef. We're going on a ride to see your uncle."

"Yes, Sir!" Josef exclaimed, and he ran to get a guard to help him.

Daniel watched from the stable. He hid in a stall when Josef entered and talked with a guard. He heard Josef ask about him but remained quiet. A tear slowly trickled down his cheek and fell on the dry straw.

Being back on the farm reminded Benjamin of better times but with new eyes he saw how run down it had become. "Definitely needs work, Klaus."

His younger brother looked around the barn. "Where do we begin? This barn needs so many repairs. The walls are solid stone, but the woodwork inside is deteriorating. The thatched roof is not in great shape either."

"We have the right men at the palace to help us," Benjamin shared.

"The detainees?" Klaus' body shuddered.

"Yes, I understand they are quite capable. Of course, there will be guards with them."

Klaus let out a sigh of relief. "Ari said to take care of the restorations while he's gone. I didn't want to start without you."

Benjamin put his arm around his brother's shoulders. "Let's make a list of the materials we need. Looks like we'll visit Papa at his work tomorrow. We'll need lots of wood."

Benjamin buried himself in his work. Josef followed his father like a shadow, enjoying every moment they worked together. When the blisters formed on his hands, he never complained. Daniel watched his constant playmate cling to his father. He didn't like seeing Joseph leave to the farm. He preferred to stay at the palace.

After the first week, Benjamin took Daniel aside. "Daniel, I need some help tomorrow at the farm. Will you come?"

"If you want me to," the boy meekly replied, lowering his head.

"I always want you around. I thought you didn't want to be with me."

Daniel looked up with tears in his eyes. "I want to be with you, but—" Daniel choked up and cried.

Tenderly Benjamin lifted Daniel's chin, "But what, Son?"

"That's it."

"What's it?"

"I want to be your son," Daniel sobbed.

Tears welled up in Benjamin's eyes. He grabbed his chest trying to pull out the pain that had ballooned inside. Lowering himself on his bended knee, Benjamin reached out for Daniel's hands. "Forgive me, Daniel. I've been so wrapped up in my grief that I didn't see yours. Daniel, from this day forward, you are my son and I am your father. There is no power on this earth that will separate my love for you."

"Just like Jesus?"

Benjamin chuckled. "Not as perfect as His love, but close."

Daniel sank into his father's embrace, letting it fill the void that existed since his parents had passed away.

Chapter 17

Hopelessness to Hope

Ari tossed and turned in bed. "Should I or shouldn't I take Ivar? Maybe the Lord will provide the answer." He yawned and went straight to sleep. The morning light slowly illuminated his room and Ari woke up.

He noticed his spare clothes were clean and neatly laid out on a chair. "That was quick." After dressing, Ari stuck his head out into the hallway. A guard noticed and motioned for him to follow.

Ari entered the dining hall. "Good morning, Papa," said Ivar.

Ari looked at his son's clothes, formal minister attire. "Seeing someone special today?"

"Yes," Ivar coyly replied.

"Uh, and do I know this person?"

"Yes."

"Are you going to tell me who it is?" Ari hopefully asked.

"King Stefan. He wants me to report on the castle's progress. We could travel together if you like."

"I like." Looking up, Ari mouthed, "Thank You."

After a quick morning meal, they guided their horses to the water. They entered the rowboat, pulling their horses after them into the river. "This bridge will be a blessing," Ivar said. "I don't know who will like it the most, people or their horses."

"Both!" Ari added.

"Ivar?"

"Yes, Papa?"

"Do you have time to go with me to see Wilhelm?"

"Why do you think I'm dressed this way?"

"What if he doesn't know where Anna and Meta are?"

"We will cross that bridge when we get there."

Several detainees had widened the path that the Hawk Man had used in the past. Travel to the city of Herrgott by horse only took one day now.

Although the building offered serene landscaping, apprehension enveloped Ari and Ivar. The last time they were in Herrgott had been joyous. Ivar and Magnus had received their ministerial ordination. Now, the unknown weighed on their minds. Knocking on Wilhelm's door, Ivar gritted his teeth.

"Ivar, what a pleasure to see you. Please come in." After Ari and Ivar sat down, Wilhelm asked, "What brings you here?"

"Rector Wilhelm, we know someone in common," Ivar began.

Frowning, Wilhelm listened with great curiosity. "Who might that be?"

"An injured woman and a baby."

Wilhelm's heart raced and his mouth went dry. "Do you know this woman and child?"

Ivar looked at his father and continued. "The woman is Meta. She is the wife of my friend in Christana."

"I know where they are!" Wilhelm exclaimed. "They're in Artz."

"They're not here?" Ari blurted out.

"No, I left the woman there. She needed medical help. The woman could never talk but took excellent care of her baby. I waited for someone to come and help her before I left Christana. When my ship arrived, she would not leave me."

Ari hung his head.

"What's wrong?" Wilhelm asked.

"My father has been searching for them. He went to Arzt, but Meta took the baby and left. No one saw her leave."

Ari looked hopefully at Wilhelm. "Do you know where she might have gone?"

"Sadly, I do not. I am so sorry."

"Thank you for taking care of them," Ari said. "We're sorry to have bothered you, Wilhelm. Let's go, Ivar."

"I'll pray for their discovery. They're somewhere." As Wilhelm walked them out, he noticed the banner Air carried in his fist. "That cross. I saw the same design on the baby's blanket."

"My Petra made them both," Ivar said. "Petra, the one with the sweet treats."

"Oh, they are good. Her mother still makes them for us."

Ari gave Wilhelm a half smile and gave his son a pleading look. "We have to go. I hope to see you soon," Ivar said.

"My door is always open. Godspeed, and I'll pray for your friend's family."

Outside, Ari kicked the pavement. "My family, my granddaughter. I can't even say that it's my granddaughter I'm looking for."

"It's time to see Stefan," Ivar said, putting his arm on his father's shoulder.

Quietly, they walked their horses to the palace. The guards on duty didn't know either Ari or Ivar and they had to wait while permission was granted. A servant came to the gate and escorted them to the king.

From the look on Ari's face, Stefan knew the visit did not contain good news. He stood up and dismissed the servant. "Ari, Ivar, come walk with me." Stefan guided the men to a quiet area in the garden.

"Stefan," Ari began. Tears welled up in his eyes. His throat tightened causing his voice to choke. Ivar patted his hand and spoke for him.

"Stefan, we found the gentleman that took care of Anna and Meta."

"Why the long faces then?"

"Since Meta could not speak and wouldn't leave the man, he took her to the University of Medicine in Arzt."

"Good, and Anna? Is she alright?" Stefan asked.

"Yes, and no." Ivar replied. Leaning forward, Stefan threw Ivar an odd look.

Ari straightened up. "I went to Arzt. Meta and the baby left without anyone knowing where they went."

"Where is this man that left my great-granddaughter alone? I want to see him, now!"

Ivar sighed. "He's the Head Master, Rector Wilhelm, at the Ministry University."

Stefan slumped back into his chair. He closed his eyes and quietly meditated. "That's it!" Ari and Ivar looked inquisitively at Stefan. "The last known town where Anna and Meta were seen was Arzt. We'll set up a search starting there and branch out from that town. Ari, your Herrgott is good, but my men can speak it better. I'm sure you'll want to go with them."

"Yes! When can we leave?"

"Tomorrow. I'll have my guards get the supplies ready. Ivar, how is that bridge coming along?"

"We hope to start laying stones for the curve very soon. The Head Architect is laying out the wooden frame for the arch over the river."

"How are the detainees doing?" Stefan probed further.

"Gunther and I call them craftsmen now. The men respond positively. It's more humane."

"Any other new developments?"

Ivar momentarily looked sideways, visualizing the work area by the river. Thinking of something to add, he said, "I had the craftsmen build a permanent structure near the bridge site."

Stefan lowered his head and asked, "And what is the nature of this structure?"

"It's for them to use when it gets cold. It has a fireplace so the workers can warm up and continue the work on the bridge during the winter. We use it to cook their meals there, too. It contains some modest furniture for the men to use while eating and resting up."

Stefan listened, his scowl deepened, but he never commented. Ivar's gut turned a little. *I hope I didn't overstep my authority at the castle.*

"Gentlemen, it's almost time for the evening meal. Let's go inside."

The horse snorted, watching his owner come into view. Ari reached out his hand and rubbed the long neck. "Good morning, boy. Are you ready to go?" The horse bobbed his head as if he knew what that meant.

Ari took inventory of his traveling companions: six uniformed guards and his son. "Let's go, Ivar. At least we'll be together today. Tomorrow, the new search begins."

Ivar turned to his father. Making sure the guards were out of hearing range, he asked. "Did you notice something different about Stefan?"

"Yes, but I can't quite tell what it is."

"Good, I thought it was just me. Let's pick up the pace. I'm eager to see Petra again."

"I know the feeling," Ari quietly mouthed. "I still miss you, Johanna." Ari's eyes started to water and he turned his head away from Ivar.

Ari's confidence boosted as he traveled with the guards. Their knowledge of the language made the search easier. He noticed an occasional stifled grin when he mispronounced a Herrgott word.

Harvesters gathered around the Kirsche trees. The red cherries hanging on the branches made his mouth water. "Want some?" one of the guards asked. Ari nodded.

The guard returned with a bag of delicious fruit that was passed around. By the time the group reached the university building, the bag was empty.

The Head Guard accompanied Ari into the building. The woman in front recognized Ari and immediately left to summon Fritz. When the physician arrived, he cautiously eyed the guard and nodded in respect. "Ari, have you found your loved ones?"

"Not yet. We're starting a wider search. I just wanted to see if you have any news about Meta."

"Unfortunately, nothing. We have asked around town, too." Fritz scanned the guard's clothing and the sword hanging by his side. "Is Meta related to our king?"

"No," Ari truthfully answered. "King Stefan allowed his guards to accompany me as a courtesy to King Albert of Christana. Meta and the baby are from Christana."

"We are at your disposal," Fritz said, nodding again.

"Thank you. We'll ask around the town and make plans to branch out from here. She went somewhere from this building and it wasn't south to the river." Ari nodded and followed the guard toward the door.

"Perhaps, Meta got her surroundings confused and rode a different way out of the city," Fritz said.

Ari twirled around on his heel. His eyes bulged at this new thought. "We will investigate that idea. Thank you."

The guards huddled together. One pointed his finger down the closest street. Another one pointed toward the opposite direction. Another pointed the way they had arrived. They departed in pairs. The guard in charge took Ari with him.

One after another, shop owners and customers shook their heads. No one remembered seeing a woman and baby on a horse. The sun faded behind the clouds and dusk settled in. The guards regrouped in front of the University. Frustrated, Ari raised his fist in the air, clutching his banner. It caught the eye of a student entering the building.

"Interesting design you have there," the student said.

Ari's heart pounded so hard he could hear the beats reverberate in his ears. "Have you seen it before?"

"Yes, it was on a baby's blanket."

"Where did they go?"

The young man pointed east. "That way, Sir."

"Did she continue on that road?"

"I don't know," the young man replied. "After I helped the woman with her baby, I went into the building."

"You did well, thank you." New hope rose up in Ari. Turning to the guards, he noticed their tired looks, but they didn't complain. "Let's spend the night here and leave in the morning."

Chapter 18

New Student

Magnus gazed into Angela's eyes. "I wish I could draw. I would make a picture of you that I could keep here at the church." Angela felt her cheeks warming up.

You always say the sweetest things. Maybe you could learn," Angela said and winked.

"Speaking of learning, Lars is getting along in his years." Angela tilted her head and frowned, not following the train of thought. "I can't play the organ, and I don't have time to learn."

Angela's eyes sparkled. "I could learn to play the organ."

Magnus' eyes glimmered. "I was hoping you would say that."

"When can I start?"

"I'll ask when I see him today."

For the rest of the day, notes of her favorite hymns wafted in Angela's mind. She sat down at the table and pretended to play the organ while she hummed the notes. Benjamin and Klaus peered through the window. "Does this mean we have to sing for our food today?"

Angela's face flushed and turned toward the window. "Just practicing. The food is ready. Come on in."

Magnus arrived shortly after "the recital" with a big grin on his face. "He said yes?" Angela asked.

Magnus slightly dipped his head. "He would be honored to share his love of playing the organ."

"When can I begin?"

"Today, if you're not busy."

Angela took her apron off and looked at the two brothers. "Benjamin and Klaus, you two can clean up today. I'm off duty." She went to her room and freshened up.

The young boy that normally pumped the organ was in the fields helping his father. Magnus had to do the honor while Lars introduced the names of the keys. "This one is C, the next one is D, the next one is–?" Lars paused.

"E," Angela excitedly announced. "This one is F. This one is G, and this one is–"

"A," Lars quickly interrupted. "And the next one is B. Now the pattern repeats."

A smile slowly creeped across Angelica's face as she correctly repeated the pattern all the way to the end of the keyboard. "I get it," she triumphantly declared.

"Get what?" a voice asked from the back of the church.

"Petra!" Angela yelled. She faced her teacher. "Excuse me, Maestro." Lars winked and Angela ran to the back of the church.

"Hello, Angela," greeted Ivar. Out of the corner of his eye, he watched his brother emerging from the back of the organ. Shaking his head, Ivar stared at Magnus. "I've only been out of town for a few months and you're demoted to the organ pumper. What did you do?"

"Come here, Ivar. Have some respect for your older brother."

"Just by a few minutes, Magnus," Ivar chided.

Ivar noticed how much Lars had changed since he had been away. His hair seemed whiter and his midsection wider—or had it always been that way? "How are you, Lars?"

"Doing well. The detainees bless my days. They are hungry to learn about the Bible. Just about all of them have been baptized and come to church services. The last two are close to making the decision for Christ."

"It sounds like you have a different kind of student," Petra noted.

"Yes, today is Angela's first lesson."

"I know the names of the keys," Angela proudly said, lifting her head up high.

"Like 'Johann,' 'Magnus,' and 'Petra'?" Ivar teased.

"They go by letters not people's names, you silly man," Angela responded. Then, she turned serious. "You're not here to talk about music. What has happened?"

Ivar pursed his lips and nodded several times. "I have news from Father." All eyes weighed heavily on Ivar and waited for his next words. "Father has found the city where Meta and Anna were taken to. A place where Meta could get medical help." Turning to Magnus, Ivar continued, "The man who was with them is Wilhelm from our University in Herrgott."

Magnus' eyes sparkled. "That's good news. He will take care of her. How is Meta and Anna?"

Ivar frowned. He took a deep breath and continued, "Somehow, Meta left the medical school with Anna and rode away. We don't know where she went, neither does Wilhelm."

Lars gasped. His legs wobbled, forcing him to sit down in the pew.

"Where's Father now, Ivar?"

"In Artz. King Stefan sent six guards with him to search the area where Meta and Anna were last seen."

"Does Johann know?" asked Angela.

"I haven't seen him yet. I'm going there now," Ivar replied. "Magnus, come with me."

Looking at his betrothed, Magnus asked, "Angela, please stay here with your cousin. We'll call for you later." Angela reached for Petra's hand.

The guards recognized Johann's brothers and quickly sent word to the prince. Johann and Tea met them in the courtyard. Their soulful looks spoke volumes. Johann squeezed Tea's hand. "Remember Psalm 100." He then addressed the two men, "Brothers, good to see you. What news do you bring?"

"Let's sit down first. I've been riding many hours."

"Of course." Johann led them to a quiet spot in the garden.

Ivar shared all the information he knew. Johann's knuckles turned white as he listened about his missing daughter, but Tea remained calm.

"My grandfather has a good plan. My daughter is in safe hands and they will be found," Tea confidently replied.

Magnus and Ivar marveled at Tea's composure. She noticed. "The Lord does His best work through our thanksgiving and praise, but most of all, through our faith. I can see it no other way."

"Did Petra come with you, Ivar?" Johann asked.

"Yes, she and Angela are in the church."

"We'll send for them. All of us are together and that's something to be thankful for," Johann said lightly squeezing Tea's hand.

"When do you return to Taulbe Castle?" Tea asked.

"I was thinking tomorrow, but I want to see the farm," Ivar replied.

"You will see a few changes, Brother," Magnus said.

"Changes?" Ivar asked.

"You'll see in the morning. It will be dark when we get home."

A good night's rest in grandma's old cottage brought back warm memories. Ivar sighed, then his stomach growled. "Hurry up, Magnus. Let's go see the changes." Ivar's eyes widened when he got closer to the farm. New thatching covered the barn's roof. The interior had been gutted and the stalls were being rebuilt.

"Placing stones on the floor would take too long, so we decided against it," Magnus said.

A loud neigh perked up Ivar's ears, and he went to the back door. "Edelrosses! I had no idea that they were here," Ivar remarked.

"You need to come home more often, Brother." A small cloud of dirt drifted in the air from the path. "Here comes baby brother, right on time."

Journey in the Waiting

Clang, clang, clang went the bell. Ivar looked oddly at Magnus.

"Our new meal-time announcement—very audible if you're in the field."

Smiling faces greeted the hungry brothers when they entered the cooking room. Eggs, salted pork, and the aroma of warm bread greeted their eyes, noses, and watering mouths. Ivar reached over to get a small piece of crust. Angela nudged his arm. They all waited until Benjamin and Klaus could join them.

"May I?" asked Johann.

Everyone nodded.

"Jesus, we thank You for this food. It came from Your earth to nourish us. We thank You for the food that is nourishing our loved ones who are not here with us. We give thanks to You for taking care of them. Most of all, we thank You, Lord, for who You are—*not* just for what You can do for us. We praise Your holy Name. Amen.

"Amen," the others repeated.

"Benjamin, how is Josef?" Ivar asked.

"He is doing very well considering the circumstances." Benjamin set his fork down and let his face glow. "He's excited about having a new brother."

Ivar pulled his head back. "Brother?"

"Daniel. We have adopted him. He's my son."

The others smiled already, knowing about Benjamin's growing family.

"We're happy for you," Petra said. "We hope to have sons one day, too."

"They are the joy of life. You'll be great parents," Benjamin shared.

"Speaking of joy, let's eat this delicious food and go work with the Edelrosses," Johann added.

"Johann, have you ever considered training the horses to perform in front of people?" Benjamin asked. "They are too magnificent for only a few to enjoy."

"Interesting proposition," Johann said. "Let me think about it."

Chapter 19

Good News, Bad News

Gunther reread his letter to Stefan. Satisfied with the contents, he folded it. Lighting the end of the wax stick, he let several drops of molten wax puddle over the edge of the folded parchment. Quickly, he lowered his seal into the wax before it solidified. The letter read:

> *My Gracious King of Herrgott*
> *Greetings Stefan,*
> *I pray you are in good health. I am in your debt and truly appreciate the position I have here at Taulbe Castle. Ivar has been a Godsend to me. His calm and sincere manner has led our detainees to be productive staff and craftsmen.*
> *The work on the bridge is progressing quickly. Working both sides of the river at the same time has hastened the project. The stone towers that are the foundation for the future arch is halfway built. We have talented men who will be good independent stone masons once the project is finished. They observe the master masons and model their examples.*
> *The men with carpentry skills have completed the construction for the frame for the arch. Soon, it will be partially dismantled and parts of it will be hoisted next to the stone foundation. After the partial wooden arch is in place, the stone masons can start the masonry work on the bottom curve of the arch. Leaving part of the support frame off will allow the river vessels to pass. When the traffic stops due to the river freezing over, we*

will add the rest of the wooden frame and wait for spring to lay the stones and complete the arch. The bridge will be functionable with the temporary wooden structure.

Unfortunately, the river will be closed until we finish the entire width of the arch. We have alerted everyone using the river. Once the mortar has set, the dismantling of the wooden frame will begin, and all vessels will be allowed passage once more.
Gunther

Stefan fumbled with the wax seal; his hands stiff in the early fall dampness. "Hmm, this is good news. I need some more good news," he muttered while thinking of his great-granddaughter.

Thoughts about baby Anna's parents stirred up memories of his own parents. "I haven't been to the library in ages. That would be a great distraction." Stefan held his head high and slowly walked down the corridor.

Light streamed through the stained-glass window and offered a slight illumination in the library. A nearby servant lit several candles. "Better," Stefan said.

Removing a book from the shelf, he noticed dust on the top of the pages. With a quick puff of his breath, the tiny particles floated in the air. "Achoo." The servant quickly came to his side, but Stefan raised his hand and waved him back.

"Ah, I haven't seen this book in a long time." Stefan settled down in a comfortable chair by the candlelight and opened the cover. He smiled as he read his family names. He slid his thumb back and forth over his son's name. "I need to record his day of death." Turning the page, he nodded several times while reminiscing about his relatives. His smile suddenly disappeared, and he slammed the book shut. "Put it back," he demanded of the nearby servant, and he left the room.

Journey in the Waiting

* * *

At first light, all the guards and Ari were ready to go, having already eaten their morning meal and packed their horses. The Head Guard took over. "We need to travel in pairs. I will go with you, Ari." Pointing to two guards, he gave the command. "You two go north." Pointing to another pair, he said, "You two go west." The last guard frowned, hoping he wouldn't be traveling alone. "Young man, I need your help. You will travel with Ari and me."

The young guard let out a sigh of relief.

The guards stopped at every shop and house they saw, working both sides of the streets and paths. No place was overlooked. The young guard stayed with Ari, who said, "You can ask the questions better than I. I'm glad you're here."

The quiet guard gave a small shrug.

After a few hours, Ari's curiosity got the better of him. "You are very dedicated in this search. Did the Head Guard say something?"

The young guard looked around, noting that his leader was out of earshot. "He didn't, but King Stefan did."

"What did he say?" Ari asked.

"If you want to keep your job, don't come back without the baby and the woman."

"We will. We will find them."

The young guard gave him an uncertain smile and knocked on another door.

"That's the last cottage on this path. Saddle up, let's get going," the Head Guard said.

Traveling down the path, the Head Guard held up his hand and stopped, "The path splits three ways. I'll take this one, and you two take that path and see where it goes. We'll meet back here by sundown."

The three separated and continued the search. The Head Guard's path slowly narrowed to just wide enough for a small wagon to maneuver in between the bushes and trees. He scanned the tree line, but saw nothing but thick woods. "No horse would choose to go in this environment," the man muttered.

* * *

Jakob walked around the cooking room, smiling and humming a familiar tune that caught Meta's attention. Smiling, she nodded her head keeping time with the melody. "I think she knows that song," Jakob remarked to his wife.

"Perhaps, or maybe she likes your humming. It could be soothing to this lost woman," Hilda replied. "Jakob, winter will be here soon. If no one comes for her, do we have enough food for all of us?"

"The Lord will provide. We had a good crop. Maybe she can help with the harvest. I need to check in on the goat. I think she went over the hill down to the creek again. Do you need more milk?" Jakob asked.

"Always. For a little girl, she has a big appetite. I need to go check in on her."

Hilda went into the baby's room, and Jakob headed to the back hill. Meta sighed, watching them walk away.

A bird flew by the cottage and landed on a nearby tree. Sweet melodies flowed from the tiny creature. Meta stuck her head out the door, looking for the bird. She edged outside to get a closer view. While focusing on the bird, a man rode up on his horse and scared the bird away.

"Good day, Madam," he said. "I am looking for a missing woman and her baby. Have you seen any strangers in this area?"

Meta couldn't understand a word he said and shook her head.

Then he pointed to the path, "Are there any more cottages down there?"

Meta quickly shook her head again. *I hope he quits talking and leaves. He looks scary in those clothes*, she thought.

"Sorry to have bothered you," he said, nodding in respect.

Meta mimicked his gesture and nodded in return.

"She's a quiet one," the guard muttered. "I'll go wait at the trail for the others. Maybe they found something."

"Hilda," Jakob yelled. "I found the goat. She was by the creek again."

"Jakob, we have a baby in the house. We must be quiet when she's sleeping."

"She doesn't sleep very long when you lay her down." Jakob winked at his wife. "I think you have spoiled her. She wants you to hold her all the time."

"I'm just thankful that the woman will let me." Hilda studied the situation. "We need to give them names. What sounds good?"

Jakob cocked an eyebrow. "I'm not touching that one. Whatever you pick, I will like."

"Hmm, a motherly name." Hilda drummed her fingers on the table. *Tap, tap, tap. Tap, tap, tap.* Closing her eyes, she saw the perfect name. "Jakob, I thought of the best name for a mother."

Jakob looked at his wife. He remained quiet and waited.

"The mother of our Lord, Maria."

"Hilda, that's a great name. Let's try it."

When Meta walked into the room, Hilda greeted her, "Maria."

Meta looked up and smiled. "She likes it!" Jakob exclaimed. "I wonder if her name is Maria." Meta looked at Jakob and smiled again.

"Now, for the baby," Hilda said. "Hmm."

"How about 'Baby'?" Jakob suggested. "Maria already has a special name for her child. We just have to wait for her to get better to tell us."

"Jakob, before winter strikes, we'll need supplies from town. I'll need cloth for my sewing."

"How much will you need?" Jakob asked.

"Let me get my supplies out. Maybe Maria can help me."

Meta stared at the cloth. She picked it up and started to measure it with her arms. Turning to Hilda, Meta made scissor movements with her fingers.

"Scissors. You want scissors?" Hilda responded imitating the cutting motion with her fingers.

Meta nodded vigorously.

Hilda pulled her sewing basket from the top shelf and brought it to the table. Meta laid the cloth on the floor. Taking a spool of thread, she unwound it and set it on top of the cloth creating an outline of a skirt.

"You can sew?" Hilda asked, making sewing motions with her hands.

Meta nodded. She picked up the scissors and held them up. Hilda nodded. Meta went to work and cut out the diagram for a skirt. She used the first cutout to make a duplicate cutout.

Her nimble fingers began to sew the pieces together. When the baby woke up, Meta motioned for Hilda to get her. Hilda drew her head backward. "Jakob, she asked me to get the baby. This sewing may help this poor woman."

By the end of the night, Meta had finished the skirt and handed it to Hilda. The woman ran her fingers over the stitches. She pulled the pieces at the seam. The stitches held tight. "Good work, Maria!" she said, smiling.

Meta beamed when part of her memory returned. *I can do this,* she thought.

"Jakob, Maria and I can make clothes this winter and sell them in spring. We'll need lots of cloth."

"Our neighbor might have that wool woven by now. I'll check with him tomorrow."

"What are we going to buy it with?" Hilda asked.

Jakob paused and studied his wife's face. "The woman's horse, maybe?" Her frowns troubled his soul. "We *are* taking care of her and her baby. Hilda, she hasn't looked at that horse since she arrived."

"I know." Hilda sighed. "It's just that she doesn't have much."

"She will next spring when we go to market with those new clothes," Jakob assured her and put his arm around his wife.

Chapter 20

Letters

The courier scanned the river bank, pulling his jacket tight around his neck in a fruitless attempt to block the wind. The water raised up in waves creating white caps at the crest. "You won't be getting wet, old boy. You're staying here." He patted his horse and tethered him to a tree. Raising his hand to his personal guard, he said, "Wait here. I'll be back shortly."

Sitting in the rowboat, the courier held his pouch close to his chest. Another gust of wind hit the water. Wiping his face, he noted, "The air is getting colder. Winter will be here before you know it." The rowing guards' mouths puckered and a few nodded politely.

Entering the castle, the courier asked for Gunther and Ivar. His head moved in every direction, taking in the architecture of the castle as he waited for the recipients. "I have a letter for each of you from King Stefan. Do you have any letters for me to take back?"

"Not at this time. You are free to return," Gunther said.

"I will wait until you have each read your letters," The courier replied.

Ivar and Gunther stared at the courier then stared at each other. Each ran their fingers over the king's wax seal and broke them. Unfolding their personal letters, they noticed that the king was brief in his request.

Gunther looked at Ivar. "This is good with me."

Ivar took longer to reply. "I have Petra to think about. I have to talk to her first."

"I understand. You are a fortunate man to have her, Ivar," Gunther said.

"Gunther, someday you will be blessed too."

Gunther gave a slight smile, but he didn't put much stock into those words. *Who would want me?* he thought, rubbing his scarred face.

"Please wait. I'll be right back." Ivar ran inside the castle.

"Petra, I need you," Ivar yelled.

"I'm in here, Ivar. What's so urgent?"

Ivar held up the letter. Petra noticed the royal seal as she turned the paper over to read it. Her eyes lit up. "Can we?"

"You want to give up what you started here?" Ivar asked.

"Both of us have started good training for the staff and craftsmen. We both would need replacements. More important is what do you want?"

"I am humbled, but it's a crucial responsibility."

Petra stepped closer. "Ivar, you are a shepherd. This flock needs you."

"Are you sure you want to do this?"

"Ivar, I'll be in my home city. The city you spent several years in, too. We won't be in a new land."

"Let's pray first." Taking Petra's hands into his own, Ivar prayed. Peace blanketed both, confirming the decision.

"Then it's agreed?" Ivar asked.

"On one condition," Petra coyly replied.

"Again?" Ivar said with a chuckle. "What's the condition?"

"I still want to teach children about God."

"Granted. Can I tell the courier now? He's waiting for a reply."

"Tell him we will be honored." Petra gave a cordial curtsey with a perky grin.

"Go tell the other women. See you later."

Tap, tap, tap went the courier's foot while he waited for Ivar. His eyes brightened when he saw the man of the cloth descending the outdoor stairs. He examined the look on Ivar's face. Ivar didn't hurry and his composure offered no clues as to his response.

Ivar glanced at his friend. Gunther read his eyes and slowly raised the corner of his mouth into a pucker.

Turning to the courier, Ivar reflected on his training and said, "Please tell His Majesty that Petra and I would be honored to accept his request."

The courier grinned and bowed. "I will relay your reply. A wagon will be sent as soon as I return to King Stefan." The courier made haste to the rowboat. His chest raised, and he let out a deep sigh. "The king has been very grumpy lately. I'm glad I have favorable news for him to hear."

Three days later, Ivar and Petra rode down the crude path in the woods to the city. The wagon, carrying their belongs, creaked behind them and occasionally hit a rut, causing the trunks of clothing to jostle around.

Petra discerned Ivar's troubled face. *He needs some cheering up. What can I do?* Turning her head, she gave a mischievous grin. "Oh no!"

"What's wrong, Petra?" Ivar asked.

"I forgot something. Can we go back?"

"Petra, we are more than halfway to Herrgott. What did you forget?"

"To say goodbye to my classroom."

Ivar rolled his eyes and shook his head. "I'm sure the room will be forgiving. Once we settle in, I'll pay a visit to Wilhelm. He will know the perfect minister for continuing your school and sharing the Gospel."

"Thank you, Ivar. I hope my students will do well with the new teacher. The other women and I were a great team, but they didn't want to stay."

"If the craftsmen have a problem, the Lord will heal it."

"We all need some healing, especially King Stefan."

The path widened when they neared Herrgott. Trees laying on their sides surrendered their branches and bark to the woodsmen's axes—foundations for new cottages dotted the landscape.

"This has dramatically changed since my last trip with my father," said Ivar. "The city is growing."

"New roads bring prosperity," Petra added.

Ivar's thoughts drifted toward his new responsibility. "I hope I don't disappoint King Stefan. He has enough on his mind."

Clomp, clomp, clomp went the sound of the horses' hooves as the path opened up to paved streets. The caravan continued to the gates of the palace.

King Stefan watched from his balcony window and saw his new guests arriving. "Lord, they're here. Thank You," he said and headed for the foyer. "Petra, welcome to my home. I have prepared a room for you, but I will understand if you want to stay with your parents."

"I haven't seen them yet. They may want to continue to be by themselves," she teasingly replied.

"Ivar, I like this woman. She has a good sense of humor."

"You're very perceptive, King Stefan," Ivar replied noting that there were guards nearby.

Stefan nodded. "Petra, I have taken the liberty to invite your parents. They are waiting in the library." Petra's eyes lit up. "While you are together, I want to show Ivar his new quarters."

Petra curtsied as Stefan guided Ivar to a different part of the palace.

***

Walking down the streets of Herrgott felt like coming home. "I can't get over how much I have missed this place," Ivar quietly muttered. Passing the local inn, he reminisced about the day he saw his father there shortly after Ari had given his life to Christ and had come to visit.

Journey in the Waiting

A small shudder traveled through Ivar's body when he thought about his encounter with the Hawk Man, who turned out to be King Stefan's wayward son. *Lord, I hope that I can give Stefan some comfort for his last remaining time here on Earth. He has suffered with the loss of his son.*

Turning the corner, Ivar saw his alma mater, the University of Ministry. A warm smile spread across his face as he entered the doorway. Making his way through the hallways, he went directly to Wilhelm's door.

Wilhelm looked up. His eyes sparkled. "Ivar, good to see you. Any news about the woman and the baby?"

The corners of Ivar's mouth drooped. "No word." Ivar's countenance changed and his face glowed. "They're someplace; we'll find them. Thank you, Wilhelm, for not abandoning them."

"That means the world to me, Ivar. I feel terrible that they are lost."

"Not lost. Someone is taking care of them just like you did."

Wilhelm nodded and sighed with relief. "What brings you to Herrgott so soon?"

"King Stefan is in need of spiritual support and asked if I would help him in his time of need."

"What of your position at Taulbe Castle?"

"That's why I'm here to see you. I need a replacement that would take care of the needs of the men there, spiritually and academically."

"Academically?" Wilhelm asked.

"Petra and her attendants have been teaching reading classes. Petra is with me, and the other women returned to Christana."

"Hmm, let me think about suitable successors to continue your accomplishments. It may take two."

Ivar tried to stifle his grin. "Thank you."

"What about Magnus?"

"He wouldn't want to leave his church. I know how he feels. It was difficult for me to leave. This is the first time we have been separated."

"After I find replacements, I'll have King Stefan give his approval."

Wilhelm studied Ivar's face. "Let me know immediately when the woman and child are found."

"I will. Thank you, Wilhelm."

Ivar whistled all the way back to the palace. His melody garnered many smiles from the city folk as they nodded passing by. When he walked into the palace gate, he stopped dead in his tracks. His eyes bulged and his jaw dropped. Coming to his senses he proceeded. "He's beautiful!" Ivar examined every detail from top to bottom of the perfectly groomed stallion tethered to the rail. Petra stood next to the white horse, rubbing his sides and head.

"He's Stefan's best Edelross," Petra said.

"Are there more?"

"Of course," she replied. "And they are looking for a trainer. Do you know of anyone who might be interested?"

Stefan, you are wise and generous. Teach me your ways, Ivar thought approaching the horse.

* * *

Tea stirred her spoon in the middle of her soup. "Mama, I feel a little apprehensive."

"Apprehensive?"

"It's been two years since I taught."

"Time goes by quickly," Maria noted.

"And the time when Anna returns is getting closer."

Maria tilted her head and smiled with her eyes. *I can learn from my daughter's faith.*

Returning to her thoughts to teaching, Tea said, "I'm going to separate Josef and Daniel in the classroom. Those two are like glue since they became brothers."

"I don't know who is worse with Daniel, his brother or his father," Albert added.

Staring at each other, they all laughed.

Tea's mind drifted away. *Anna, you will be coming home soon. Mama loves you.* Tea got up from the table and walked to the door.

Albert started to follow her, but Maria grabbed his arm. "She needs a quiet moment."

With a determined look on her face, Tea walked into the courtyard and headed for the burial area. Reaching her uncle's grave, she stopped and stared at the marker, Stefan the Younger. She drew in a deep breath. "I know what I have to do now, Lord. I couldn't do it before, but I'm ready now."

Looking at the grave site, Tea poured out her heart, "Stefan, I'm angry at you for what you did to me. I have never truly forgiven you. I did so only with empty words, but not with my heart. I am sorry. This unforgiveness is holding me captive and maybe holding up my daughter's return." Tea took a deep breath and closed her eyes. "Uncle, with all of my soul and spirit, I forgive you." Tears spilled from Tea's eyes and ran down her face and cleansed the hidden bitterness in her heart.

With one more deep breath she confessed, "Forgive me, Jesus. I'm sorry."

Tea sat down, trying to create a positive memory of a man she never knew. Her eyes twinkled and she looked at the sky. "I'll see you in Heaven, Uncle Stefan. We will have all eternity to get to know each other."

* * *

Strong winds prevailed from the north, bringing the colder air with it. Ari and the guards put on an extra layer of coats. Coming to the border of the adjacent county, they had to make a decision.

The two guards whispered to each other as they sat around the campfire. "I'm sorry that you have to be the one to tell him," the younger guard said. "He's not going to like it."

"It's my duty," the Head Guard said.

Ari lifted his head and stared at them. "You don't have to say it. I know. We need to go back."

"Maybe the other guards found them. We won't know unless we return," the Head Guard said.

Ari nodded. He threw another branch on the fire and watched the sparks fly into the air. *You're out there somewhere, Anna. Pawpaw will find you.*

* * *

Sleep eluded Gunther, and he rose before the morning light. Entering the courtyard, he reminisced about the courier who had brought his letter from Stefan. *I wonder how Ivar is doing with his new job. I miss him.*

Gunther continued his way to the top of the rampart. Leaning over the edge to try and get a better look, he noticed movement on the other side of the river. "Who could that be?" he muttered.

Out of the tree line emerged two figures, a woman with a young boy. Lowering her bundle, the woman knocked on the door of the building near the river and waited for a response. Pulling her cloak tighter around her neck, she knocked again. She pushed the door open and peered inside. Noting that it was empty, she picked up her bundle and led the boy indoors.

"Good morning, Sir," a sentry said while he patrolled the wall. "That's probably vagrants over there. Do you want me to chase them away?"

"No," Gunther replied. "Let's see what they will do first. Tell the workers to not use that building today. They can warm up in the castle when necessary. It's getting close to the time to connect the two top spans of the wooden arch. Then the craftsmen can cross from one side to the other."

Gunther continued to watch the sun shedding its morning glow on the river, revealing the first sign of winter: ice forming on the edges of the riverbank.

Chapter 21

Winter

On his better days, King Stefan sat on his throne and listened to petitioners. He only presided over the more difficult cases. Ivar sat off to one side where he could observe and contemplate the complaints from a biblical point of view.

One day, King Stefan motioned for Ivar to follow him into his chambers before making judgment on a problem concerning ownership of a horse. "Ivar, this is a difficult case. What is your opinion?"

The palm of Ivar's hands became clammy. *My opinion might have an impact on one of these men's lives.*

Stefan narrowed his eyes and stared at Ivar. "Tell me what you are thinking right now."

Ivar gasped. *I have to tell the truth!* "Stefan, my thoughts are about the impact my words may have on the people involved."

"Do the words you use from the pulpit have the same effect?"

"Yes, but this affects the people's lives here on earth."

"Do the words you use in counseling have the same effect?"

Ivar conceded. "We do not have an easy duty, do we?"

"Both circumstances are similar. The difficult part in this is knowing who is truthful and who is not."

"How can you tell?" Ivar asked.

Stefan leaned back in his chair. "I look for witnesses. If that's not available, I look for past behavior and motives."

"What about this case?"

Stefan planted his elbow on the arm of his chair and rested his chin on his fist. "What are your thoughts, Ivar?"

Ivar looked away. "The farmer needs a horse for his farm. The visitor needs a horse to travel. Both claim the horse. The one most familiar with the horse should know some identification mark on it that the other person would not know."

"Like a mark in an owner's book?"

"A good comparison," Ivar responded. "Yes."

"Then let's investigate. I could use a good walk in the fresh air. Let's go visit this animal in question."

Returning to the throne room, they called the farmer into a private chamber. The other man wrung his hands and kept staring at the door. Ivar opened the door and motioned for the visitor to come in while the farmer waited in the courtroom.

The visitor shifted his eyes back and forth from Stefan to Ivar as he described the horse.

Stefan slapped his hands on the arm of his chair. "Let's all go outside."

The king rubbed his hand over the scar on the horse's neck. Turning his head, the horse eyeballed the strange man and snorted. The visitor sported a smug smile and slowly nodded. Ivar lifted the horse's rear leg to examine his hoof and the horse neighed in protest. The visitor turned slightly pale.

"May I?" Ivar asked King Stefan.

Stefan nodded.

Ivar looked at the visitor. "Where did you have this horse shod?"

"In my village," the man replied wringing his hands again.

"How long ago?" Ivar probed further.

"A long time ago," the man indignantly replied.

"What letter does your name start with?"

Feeling queasy about the line of questions, the peddler replied. "This horse is not worth the fight. You can have him. I'll just take my saddle and go."

Stefan nodded at his guards who blocked the man's path. "Say the first letter of your name," King Stefan ordered.

"M," the visitor mumbled.

"This horseshoe is cracked," Ivar announced. "That's why the horse was tied to the fence on the farmer's property. He was going to take the horse in to have a new one put on. The blacksmith imprinted the farmer's initial in it: G. It's still visible as the shoe is barely worn."

Stefan motioned for the guards to take the visitor away.

Looking at the farmer, Stefan pronounced his verdict. "You may keep the saddle for the trouble you had to endure. You are free to go."

"Thank you, Sire. Come on, old boy," said the farmer patting his horse and leading him to the palace gate.

"Good logic Ivar."

Ivar nodded. "What will happen to the other man?"

"Sadly, he chose his own fate. The crime and punishment were documented a long time ago." Ivar threw Stefan an odd look. "The law and the appropriate consequences are recorded. We administer what is written."

"Just like the Bible, when Paul wrote to the Roman Christians that the wages of sin is death."

"But the gift of God is eternal life in Christ Jesus," Stefan added.

"You know your scriptures."

"It's important when people's lives are entrusted in my care."

"I agree. There are more cases waiting inside. Shall we go?" Ivar asked. Stefan smiled and placed his arm around the young man's shoulders.

* * *

Large snowflakes descended from the sky, landing at will on objects below. One landed on Ari's hand. The warmth of his skin melted the delicate water crystal. More flakes began to fall. He pulled his coat tighter, trying to keep his hands inside for warmth.

Two of the other guards met up with Ari's group in Arzt. They had no clues or information about the missing baby and woman. The other two guards had not returned.

"We need to return to Herrgott before it gets colder," the Head Guard said. "It may be too cold for these horses to swim across already."

"What about King Stefan's orders?" the young guard asked. "Don't return without the baby and the woman."

"We have to report our findings. That's our duty now."

Ari remained quiet. His duty haunted him. He didn't relish reporting his findings to his family and Benjamin.

The snow stopped falling, but already covered the branches and ground. Under different circumstances, the sight would be beautiful, but the weary riders trudged on, disregarding what nature had shared with them.

Smoke curled upward in the late afternoon sky, beckoning to the group like a light in the dark. The aroma of simmering food greeted them when they entered the door. The innkeeper smiled as several paying guests came in for the night.

Reaching Taulbe Castle the following afternoon, the group assessed their next task, crossing the river. They scanned the temporary wooden arch, trying to estimate if it could hold the weight of a horse.

Ari broke away from the group and went into the castle. Gunther ran through the gate and threw his arms around his friend's neck. "Ari, I have missed you." Gunther knew by the look on Ari's face and the fact that he was traveling alone that the trip was unsuccessful. He waited until Ari wanted to talk.

"Gunther, my friend, I have missed you."

"Come inside and warm up, Ari."

The Head Guard watched Ari go in the castle gate. He turned and questioned one of the craftsmen working on the wooden arch. "Can this frame hold the weight of our horses?"

"All at once, no," the craftsman replied, pointing to the frame. "One at a time when the cross-frame, lateral boards are attached, yes."

"When will that be?"

"When the river freezes and river traffic stops. Then we will install the remaining support beams."

"When will that be?" the guard probed further.

"Who can predict the weather?" the craftsman replied with a shrug. "As you can see, ice is already forming on the edges of the riverbank. You could use the rowboat and leave your horses here."

The guard puckered his mouth in thought, nodding to the worker. Looking at his fellow guards, he said, "Let's go inside and warm up."

The following morning, Ari thanked the guards for all of their help before he left for home. "We'll stay here and wait a few more days for the other two guards," the Head Guard said. "We can't take the horses. The river is too cold, and they will not survive the swim. We have to walk back."

Ari laid his hand on the guard's shoulder and quietly thanked him with a squeeze of his hand. The guard nodded in return. Getting on his horse, Ari headed north.

"No river crossing for me," Ari muttered. Thoughts of staying at the castle crossed his mind, but his heart thought of his family. "They need to know the results of our journey. I would want to know." He kept his horse moving along in the freshly fallen snow.

* * *

The town square came into view with people milling about. It reminded Ari of a more joyous time that he had encountered there: the first time he and Johanna were together. "I still miss you, Johanna. Someday, we will be together again." His chest raised up and lowered, releasing a deep sigh.

Looking at the palace gate, Ari's heart pounded. "Jesus, You are the Master Healer. Please heal our hearts. I have failed. I couldn't find them. I couldn't find my granddaughter."

Ari dismounted and went through the gate. Johann ran to his father. Looking at his son, Ari's chin trembled and he broke down sobbing. His eyes turned red as he tried to hold back the tears. "I couldn't find them. I have failed."

"You have not failed, Papa."

Ari stood back, staring at his son with a puzzled look. "But I couldn't find Anna."

"God knows where she is, and Meta is taking care of her. We will find her in the spring. We have a plan. Come inside, and I'll tell you all about it."

"Does Stefan know?" Ari asked.

"He's the one who thought of it," Johann replied. "You've been gone for a long time."

* * *

Smoke rose from the chimney of the riverside building. It's source barely warmed the interior. The woman and her son huddled close to the small flames in the hearth. "Mother, we need more sticks and branches."

"I'll gather some while you fish. Remember, stay out of the water. That current is swift," his mother warned.

"It's also cold," the boy replied. "I don't want to get wet."

Carrying his makeshift fishing pole, the boy walked down the riverbank away from the craftsmen. "Strange that they never say anything," the boy remarked. "This is has to be their building."

From the rampart ledge, Gunther watched the boy poke the ice with a tree branch opening up the fishing hole again. *Be careful child,* he thought. *Where did you come from? Why are you here?*

The new minister from Herrgott joined Gunther. "Hardworking individual."

"Huh?" Gunther replied.
"The boy over there—hardworking individual."
"Oh, I didn't notice him."
The minister didn't probe further but gave a knowing smile. "When will the craftsmen complete the wooden arch?"

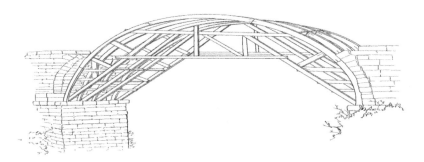

"Soon, since the river traffic has stopped," replied Gunther. "The craftsmen are working on the final braces. Then, we can send the guards' horses back."

The minister left and Gunther continued to watch the boy. *I never see a man with them. I wonder where his father is. The boy is a hardworking individual. With winter coming, they'll need more food besides fish.*

The boy's mother joined her son and tossed her fishing line into the hole in the ice. Wrapping her arm around her son, she nestled his head by her side.

* * *

Occasionally, guards from Herrgott arrived with supplies for the castle. Gunther instructed the guards to leave some food at the craftsmen's building. "Just leave the food outside. The workers will take it in later."

"As you wish," one of the guards replied and they returned to Herrgott with a lighter load on the pack horses.

Before the day was over, the food disappeared, and the assuring sign of smoke curled upward and ascended above the humble roof.

Chapter 22

Winter Ends

Gunther scrambled up the stairs to take his ritual morning walk on the rampart facing the river. He closed his eyes and faced the sun, letting the rays warm his face. Opening his eyes, he noticed the snow receding from the edges of the castle. Signs of spring flourished.

Glancing to the other side of the river, Gunther watched the boy walk to the river with his pole. "Their food supply is low or they're hungry for fish. Be careful child."

Sitting on a support board, connected to the wooden arch, the boy used a long board to jab a hole in the ice. It worked, and he dropped the board near the ice hole. The boy pulled a small piece of food from his pocket and baited the hook.

A gust of wind pushed the icy cold air into the boy's face, and he pulled his cover tighter together. His pole jerked. Did he have a bite? Pulling the pole upward, the hook got caught on the edge of the ice hole. Rolling his eyes, he lowered his body to the surface of the ice.

Gunther watched in horror, hearing the boy screaming for his mother when the ice collapsed. The boy fell into the water clinging with all his might to the board straddling over the edge of the hole. His mother came running and threw her cloak out for her son to grab.

Gunther ran down the rampart stairs, grabbing a rope in the process. He yelled to the guards and craftsmen, "Quick, follow me!" As Gunther ran to the bridge, he tied the rope to his waist. "Hold on to the end and don't let go!" he commanded the men.

Nearing the child, Gunther yelled, "Boy, look at me. Take a deep breath, I'm coming to get you." Gunther jumped in and grabbed the boy. Both went under the ice.

The slacken rope tightened, and the men strained to pull. Cheers erupted when two heads bubbled out of the ice hole. Going to the side of the riverbank, the men pulled Gunther and the boy to shore. They had to pry Gunther's nearly frozen arms off the boy.

The guards picked up the boy and Gunther, carrying them to the nearby building. The boy's mother placed more wood on the fire. She pulled the wet garments off her son and dressed him into dry clothes. The boy quivered uncontrollably as his mother wrapped a blanket around him.

The door swung open, allowing gusts of cold air to fill the room. The minister walked in and used his shoulder to shut the door while lowering the latch with his free hand. Gunther's wet clothes became even colder, and he violently shivered by the fireplace. The woman tightened her cloak around her neck.

The minister threw the woman an apologetic look. "I brought Gunther dry clothes and blankets for him and your son. Hot broth will be sent over shortly."

Gunther heard what the minister said and tried to get up, but the minister pushed his head down. The guards assisted Gunther into the dry clothes and covered him with blankets. His body continued to shake uncontrollably. The minister assessed the situation. "Going outside in that bitter cold in his current condition is not recommended. He needs to stay near this warm fire, Madam. He is not well." The minister looked around the humble surroundings that the mother and child lived in. "I'll return with more wood and food and stay with you tonight."

The woman thought about having two men alone with her and her son. *One is ill and the other is a man of God. I should be safe.* "Thank you for your help. I am Carina." She pronounced it kah-REE-nah. "My son is Isaak." She pronounced it EE-zahk.

Gunther heard the names but suffered from confusion. "Where am I?" he asked.

"You're in a safe place," the minister told him. "Try to get some sleep." Gunther closed his eyes and didn't open them until the following morning.

When morning arrived, Carina noticed her guest's eyes slowly opening. "You're awake, Gunther," Carina said. "Are you hungry?"

Gunther tried to lift his body, but his head swirled, making him dizzy, so he laid back down. "Where am I?"

"The other side of the river," the minister spoke up. "You had a rough night."

Snippets of memory came back. "The ice. The boy! Is he okay?"

"Yes, thanks to you," Carina said. "You saved his life. He is over there resting."

Gunther looked at the small frame of the child covered by the blanket. "Thank God."

"Ahem." The minister cleared his throat. "I need to check on something in the castle. I'll be back soon." When the door opened, a gust of cold air barreled into the room.

Carina pulled her cloak tighter around her neck. "Are you the one to thank for all the food this past winter?" she asked.

Gunther's face reddened.

Guessing it was him, she continued, "Thank you. You've been very kind." She propped Gunther up and brought him a bowl of broth.

He stared at her hand when she sat in the chair next to him. "If I may ask, what happened?" He nodded at her hand.

"A fire in my parents' home. I burned it trying to rescue them." Rubbing her very scarred hand, she slowly lowered her head. "They died in that fire."

Gunther looked at the ring on her other hand, "Where is your husband?"

Taking a deep breath, she shared her story. "I married a man that I thought would take care of me, but after our son was born, he became restless. A year ago, he ran off with scoundrels and was killed. The villagers were sympathetic, but the memories in that village were too painful, so we left."

One at a time, tears escaped her eyes and rolled down her face. "When I found this place, I had to stop running. My son needed a shelter."

Gunther's heart ached to touch her hand. "I have a scar, too," Gunther said, tracing his finger across his beard line.

"How did you get it?"

"I resisted an evil from an evil man, but yours is different. It was for doing good for good people."

A knock came on the door. "Come in," Carina invited.

The minister set more food on the table. "Gunther, you're sitting up. Are you ready to leave?"

"I would like to stay a little longer until the boys wakes up."

"Just signal the sentry and someone will come to help you. Good day, Madam." With a nod of his head, the minister left.

Carina reached out and touched Gunther's hand. "Thank you."

Gunther laid his hand on top of hers.

With his eyes open and facing the wall, Isaak began to talk in his sleep, "Papa. I want a Papa." Carina went to her son's side, and he pretended to wake up. "Mama."

"Are you feeling better, Isaak?"

"Much better now that you met the man from the rampart."

"Young man, you and I need to talk," Gunther said sternly.

Isaak's eyes opened wide and watched Gunther slowly raise up and come his way. "I need to ask you something." The boy continued to stare at the tall man. "May I have your permission to call upon your mother?"

Isaak looked at his mother. She nodded. He returned his stare at Gunther and nodded, too. "Yes, Sir."

"We can do things together, too," Gunther added in a softer voice. "We could go fishing."

"Not for a while, if you don't mind."

Gunther chucked. "Good idea." Turning to Carina, Gunther took her scarred hand in his. "Isaak may recover better at the castle. Shall we take him there?"

Carina leaned into Gunther, and he wrapped his arms around her. His prayer had been answered. Looking up he mouthed, "Thank You, Jesus."

* * *

One by one, the courier delivered his letters. Tea read hers first. "It's time," Tea announced. "Get our guards ready. Grandpa is sending his search party to the castle."

Ari read his letter. His face betrayed his feelings. "What's wrong, Papa?" Johann asked.

"I won't be going with the guards. Stefan has requested me to come to Herrgott." Ari let out a large sigh of disappointment.

"The guards that rode with you know where to concentrate their search," Johann pointed out.

"That's true, but I want to be there with them. I have to do something."

"You will do something—going to Herrgott."

"At least I'll get to see Ivar." Ari packed his things.

* * *

Gunther welcomed the new arrivals. Carina and Isaak stood by his side. Spotting Ari, Gunther yelled, "Ari, come here."

A smile spread across Ari's face. "I told you it would happen."

Carina threw Gunther an odd look. Gunther hastened to say, "Ari, this is Carina and Isaak."

"Do you like horses, young man?" Ari asked.

"Yes!" Isaak replied.

"Then you are one fortunate boy. This man will share his knowledge with you." Looking at Carina, Ari said, "Pleased to meet you, Madam." Turning to Gunther, he added, "You are one blessed man, my friend." Ari gave Gunther pat on his arm. "I wish I could stay longer, Gunther, but I'm going to Herrgott tomorrow."

The Head Guard, standing next to them, interrupted, "Gunther, King Albert gave strict orders for us to leave at first light with the Herrgott guards." He handed Gunther a parchment. "This was printed last week. We have a large bundle of them."

Gunther unrolled the parchment and read it out loud. Carina gasped. Gunther lovingly gazed into her eyes. "Carina, this does not pertain to you. You are covered."

* * *

Several torches illuminated the courtyard. First light had barely appeared. Gathering their horses, the guards headed for the river path. The Head Guard from Herrgott had been down this

Journey in the Waiting

path a few months ago. This time, his mission took on a different direction.

Holding a paper in one hand, the Head Guard entered the inn by the river. "May I help you?" the innkeeper asked.

"I have orders from King Stefan to nail this proclamation on every inn, shop, and establishment in Herrgott."

"Please do, Sir."

The guard nodded and nailed the document next onto the doorframe. "The parchment remains until further notice."

The innkeeper hurried to his door as soon as the guard left.

Attention Citizens
By the Decree of King Stefan of Herrgott
and
King Albert of Christana
All children under the age of 15 who have lost their fathers
are required to be escorted to the Church of Christana near the palace.
Special assistance will be offered for the mothers and their children
and children without any parents.

Chapter 23

Spring

Rows of baby beds lined one of the walls in the church. The other wall had beds for older children. Stacks of blankets rested on the pew. Crossing his arms and laying them on his rotund midsection, Lars eyed the crowded church with great anticipation. "We're going to help so many people in their time of need."

Magnus joined him. "I can't imagine what Johann and Tea must be feeling right now. Their daughter might be found in one of these beds."

"Don't forget Benjamin," Lars added. "His wife might be standing next to Anna. We'll recognize Meta, but the baby will be almost one. That's a big change in a child's life."

"Praise God. He's providing."

* * *

"Goodbye, Ma'am, see you next week," the children said.

Tea watched her students, one by one, leave her room. "They're gone." She quickly dashed to the window hoping to catch a glimpse of someone walking toward the church.

"Do you see anyone?" a voice asked behind her.

Tea twirled around to see Josef staring at her. "Not yet, Josef. Let's go for a walk." Passing Anna's room, Tea paused. Taking a deep breath, she opened the door.

"I haven't been in here for a long time," Josef recalled. "Not since Anna and Momma left."

Holding Josef's hand, Tea walked him over to Anna's cradle. "Anna's last night was difficult for her. She was so fussy about sleeping. We had to put several cloths down before she could fall asleep." Tears welled up in Tea's eyes. "Let's go, Josef. Daniel will be looking for you."

Josef reluctantly left Anna's room. He narrowed his thoughts to that last night with Anna. *What happened that night?* Then his eyes brightened. "Ma'am, I'm a little tired. Could you keep Daniel busy while I rest?"

"Sure, I'll take him to the library. He loves for me to read him a story."

"Thank you, I'll see you at meal time." Josef walked toward his room and stopped.

"No one's looking," Josef assured himself peeking down the hallway. He tiptoed all the way back to Anna's room. He lifted up all of the cloths out of cradle. A huge smile spread across his face as he carefully laid the cloths back.

Josef entered his room and headed straight for his wardrobe. "Where is that old box?" he mumbled scanning the shelves. Pure determinations fueled his quest. "There it is!" His hands grasped the box and opened the lid. Rummaging through his old clothes, he found his jacket, the one he had worn the night before Anna left with his mother. Reaching into the pocket, he retrieved his prize. Carefully, he replaced his jacket and set the box back in the wardrobe.

* * *

Guiding his horse over the wooden arch, Ari contemplated his meeting with Stefan. "Maybe it's another strategy if this new one doesn't work," Ari muttered. His horse eyeballed him and bobbed his head. Ari chuckled. "Thanks, I needed a good laugh."

Stefan met Ari in the palace. "Where's Ivar?" Ari asked.

"He's working with the Edelrosses right now. Come sit. We haven't had time to talk for a while." Stefan shared his thoughts and proposed plan with Ari.

Ari got out of his chair and walked to the window. He saw Ivar in the distance. Turning around, he closed his eyes and shook his head. "I'm too old to do this."

"I understand. Let's go find your son."

The following day, Ari headed back to the castle. Entering the gate, he wondered, *That's odd; Gunther is usually here to greet me.* Looking toward the stable, he saw Gunther with a finely dressed man.

"Ari, come on over," Gunther yelled.

The other man turned around and smiled.

Ari gaped at the visitor. "Wilhelm, good to see you."

"Good to see you, Ari. I've been admiring these beautiful horses," Wilhelm said.

"They are beauties. I miss working with them," Ari admitted.

"You can train these horses?"

"Yes, you're talking to my teacher right here."

Gunther rolled his eyes, "We taught each other a few lessons. Ari, are you staying long?"

"No, I'll leave at first light."

"May I travel with you?" Wilhelm asked. "I haven't seen my colleague Lars since he left the University."

"Of course. He has had an important impact on my life."

"How's that?" Wilhelm asked.

"He led me to a personal relationship with Jesus; then he baptized me."

"He did the same for me," Gunther added.

Wilhelm marveled at their testimonies. He puckered. *I miss sharing the Gospel with the flock.*

* * *

Hilda counted the pieces of clothing that she and her house guest had sewn during the winter. "Jakob, we have never had this many skirts, jumpers, and pants. What if the shopkeeper will not buy them all?"

"We'll find another shop," he replied. "With the profits from the clothing, we can save for our future. The farm work is getting more taxing to do, and we have to think about the baby's future."

"How long will you be gone?"

"If I leave at sunup, maybe two days, more if I go to another village," he replied.

"Jakob, you shouldn't travel alone," Hilda warned.

"Who will take care of the farm if you go?"

"Take Maria. She won't leave her baby and I can't take care of the baby and the farm by myself."

"I don't like it, but there is safety in numbers. One thing for sure, it's going to be quiet. Maria still lacks speech."

At sunup, Jakob fastened the last rope crisscrossing the cart. He left a small area for the child to ride. With a final wave to Hilda, Jakob pulled the donkey's reins and the group headed for town.

By late afternoon, the small caravan arrived in Arzt. Jakob made haste to the shopkeeper's door. "Hello, Jakob," the shopkeeper greeted. "What do you have this year?"

"Too many to carry in. Come outside."

The shop keeper's eyes bulged. "Did you help Hilda sew this time? You have so many."

"We had help." Jakob replied, and he pointed to his helper. She's helping me while Hilda takes care of the farm."

"I'll take some, but I don't need all of the garments." The shopkeeper selected the ones he needed and piled them in Jakob's arms. "Come inside, and we'll settle up the bill."

Jakob smiled while he counted his coins and placed them in his pouch. As he walked out the door, he passed a parchment nailed to the doorframe. "I wonder what that says."

The shopkeeper came back outside. "Jakob, it's getting dark. Would you like to store your wares here in the shop? I have a spare room for the woman and child. You could sleep in the shop."

"Thank you. You are very kind."

Meta looked at Jakob with apprehension when he led her to the room. She remembered the last time that happened; the kind man had left her. This time, she pointed to the floor for him to sleep there. He nodded and laid the clothing on the wooden floor to create a softer bed.

In the morning, the shopkeeper returned with three bowls of porridge which were quickly consumed. "Which way do you suggest I go to sell my wares?" Jakob asked.

"Head straight out of town pass the kirsche trees and cross over the main road to the new path. It leads to another new path. Go north."

After packing up his wares, Jakob led his group to the new path.

* * *

"There's the church," Ari announced. "Magnus and Lars are going to be surprised to see you."

The doors of the church swung open and three small children walked out. Magnus was right behind them. Looking up, he noticed his father. "Papa, it's good to see you. It has started."

Looking past his father, Magnus saw his university rector. "Wilhelm!" Magnus raised his arms up. "Very good to see you."

"How many children are here?" Ari anxiously asked.

"Just these three," Magnus answered. "They wanted to play outside."

"Where will all these children go once the search is over?" Wilhelm asked.

"That's a good question. If you have some suggestions, please share."

"Lars inside?" Wilhelm asked.

"Yes, but he's counseling the mother of these children."

"Magnus, I'm going out to the farm. I'll see you tonight," said Ari. "Wilhelm, God bless your stay and journey back home."

Wilhelm nodded and Ari quickly guided his horse down the familiar path, sporting a big smile. "My own bed tonight." Looking up at the sky, Ari's smile faded. "Lord, when should I carry out my next mission?"

* * *

The following day, more children showed up with their mothers. Some had no parents at all and were brought by citizens that were honoring the decree. Josef roamed the church looking for his mother. Johann squeezed Tea's hand as they met each mother. Their eyes anxiously examined each child. A boy, nearly one year old, raised his head and pointed his finger toward Tea, admiring her shiny locket.

Josef hovered over the beds for the one-year-old children. He meticulously arranged the blankets for maximum comfort. Then, he prayed over each bed. Looking at the bigger beds, he closed his eyes and took a deep breath. "They need prayers, too."

* * *

The sun dipped below the horizon. Lit torches lined the streets aiding the occasional townsfolk as they headed home. Jakob entered the square, almost dragging his exhausted donkey behind him. He couldn't read, but his nose detected food, and he followed the trail to the inn. He held up two fingers and pointed to the room sign.

"No rooms," the innkeeper replied.

Jakob shook his head and pointed to his companions. "Maria and baby."

Journey in the Waiting

The innkeeper detected his Herrgott accent and pointed to the church. "Kirche."

Jakob nodded and left.

Jakob knocked, and the door slowly opened. One of the mothers from inside put her finger to her mouth, "Shh." She pulled the baby's blanket back to assess the age of the child and then waved the group in. Darkness filled the sanctuary, limiting their visibility.

They put Anna in one of the baby beds. Meta laid down on the pew not far away. The woman in charge escorted Jakob to the front of the church. The helping mother waved goodbye and closed the door in his face.

"I guess I'm sleeping outside tonight. Come donkey, let's go find you some grass to eat."

Rays of sunlight streamed through the stained-glass windows. The women began to attend to the children. Meta started to accompany one of the women to where the food was kept. She paused, staring at the altar which had a ray of light directly bathing the cross on the wall.

Josef pushed the door open and peeked inside. "A new baby came last night," he whispered.

Anna stood up in her bed. She cried and balled up her fist to rub her eyes. Josef and Daniel walked over to her crib.

Out of the corner of his eye, Daniel noticed the other boys from the woods were waving at him. "I'll be right back, Josef."

Josef patted his brother on the back. Turning to the baby, he tried to comfort her. "I miss my Mama, too."

Meta turned her head from the cross toward the boy, recognizing his voice. "Josef?"

Benjamin came in the front door, looking for his son. When he walked down the aisle, Josef screamed, "Mama?"

Benjamin looked up, "Meta?"

She responded, "Benjamin?"

Benjamin ran to his wife. Meta's hands trembled as Benjamin took her into his arms. Her knees gave way, slipping through his embrace, and crumbled to the ground. Benjamin sat beside her holding her hands. "Meta, I have searched for you in Christana and Herrgott, but I couldn't find you anywhere. I'm so sorry."

"Benjamin, the Lord provided, and I'm home."

Josef rushed to his mother's side. "Mama. You're home. Did you find the medicine for Anna?"

Meta pulled her son into her lap, wrapping her arms around him. Perceiving his request, she answered, "Her medicine was found."

"Mama, I have a new brother, Daniel."

Meta pulled her head back and gave Benjamin a confused look.

"I found him while looking for you. He had no family. Daniel come closer, Son."

Daniel inched his way to Meta. She patted her other leg. "Come, Daniel." He smiled and hugged his new forever mother.

A servant immediately ran to the palace. "Meta is in the church," he yelled.

Johann and Tea locked eyes and rushed to the church. They searched the small beds looking for their Anna. A little girl was fussing and rubbing her eyes. Tea turned around and instinctively picked her up to help quiet the child while she continued to look at all the baby beds for a smaller baby. Laying the babe on her shoulder she talked sweetly and patted the baby's back.

Ari and Magnus walked in. When Tea turned to look toward Meta. Ari saw the little girl's face. *That's her hair, her eyes.* His jaw dropped and his mouth went dry. "Johanna!" he yelled.

Tea frantically looked at the other baby beds. "Where, Ari?"

"In your arms!"

Tea slumped to the floor caressing her daughter. Lowering the child to see her face, the baby looked at Tea and said, "Ma-

Journey in the Waiting

ma." Then, the little girl laid her head on her mother's shoulder, and the overly tired little girl fell fast asleep.

Josef kissed his mother on the forehead and scrambled to Anna's bed. He retrieved the pea out from under the blanket in the bed and held up for all to see. "Remember when Anna's rattle broke the night before she left. One of the peas rolled under her blanket and it bothered her. So, I put one in every baby bed here. It's the same pea that bothered the princess!" He picked up the old blanket that Petra had made and brought it to Tea.

Tea looked at Josef. She rubbed her fingers on the edges of the stitched cross. "Thank you, Jesus. You brought my baby back home."

Jakob entered the church. He looked at all the finely dressed people hovering over Meta and the baby. Meta walked over to him and took his hands. "Thank you."

"She can talk!" Jakob stared at the woman. "You can talk! Who are you?"

Meta gave Benjamin a confused look and he quickly translated the words. The grateful woman pressed her hand to the bottom of her neck. "I'm Meta." With her free arm, she waved it around. "My home, Christana."

Jakob understood a few of those words, and he shook her hand. "Good, good."

Benjamin placed his hand on Jakob's shoulder and spoke in his language, "Thank you for taking care of my Meta and the baby."

"She's not yours? Who does the baby belong to?" Jakob asked.

"She's ours," Johann replied. "Thank you for taking care of her."

Jakob's eyes scanned up and down, examining Johann's and Tea's clothes. "A princess! I had a princess in my home. Wait until Hilda hears about this."

"How can we pay you in return?" Tea asked softly cradling her sleeping baby.

"I could use a horse for my farm. I do have coins," Jakob said.

"Done," Ari interjected. "I have a good horse for you."

Johann placed his hand on Jakob's shoulder. "You took care of my daughter's needs. Now, I will take care of your needs for the rest of your life."

Albert and Maria rushed in. Their eyes scanned the room and landed on Tea. "There's Tea," Maria said, pointing.

"She has Anna!" Albert remarked as they walk up to their granddaughter. "Thank You, Lord. You brought her back."

Josef lightly slid his hand on Anna's head. "Sleep well, Anna. You're home."

Wilhelm and Lars watched the family from a distance. "Perhaps this is the Lord's timing. I hope Magnus agrees," Wilhelm said.

"We'll soon find out. Let's give the family time rejoice before we ask," added Lars.

* * *

Magnus looked at his father carefully. His morning meal churned in his gut. Pacing the dirt floor in the barn, he contemplated the news. "Does Ivar know?"

Ari watched his son with an analyzing eye. "No."

Magnus gulped. "Let me think about it. I have to get back to the church."

Ari placed his hand on his son's shoulder. "Have Wilhelm and Lars pray with you."

Magnus nodded and left for town. An invisible dark cloud hovered over Magnus, robbing him of any form of peace. He tried to pray, but the words stuck in his throat. "What are You trying to tell me, Lord?"

Entering the church, he sought after Lars, but Wilhelm motioned for him. "Magnus, I need you."

Magnus let out a small sigh of frustration and followed Wilhelm down the hall. "Magnus, I have an offer for you." Magnus tilted his head slightly. "These past few months have been weighing on my mind, and I have prayed many times. Each time the Lord has given me peace."

Magnus thought about his prayer. *Peace eluded me today in my prayer.*

"I want to return to my original training."

Magnus frowned. Deep furrows filled his forehead.

"I want to resign my office and offer you a teaching position at the University. If you agree, I will take your position here. Lars and I will pastor this church."

Relaxing, Magnus' whole body flooded with total peace. "This is an honor, Wilhelm. I must talk with Angela, first."

"We have already sent for her," Wilhelm added.

When Angela entered the church, she stopped to admire the children. Magnus and Wilhelm watched her interact with the little ones. "Angela, over here," Magnus called.

Angela looked up and smiled. As she walked closer, she noticed the glow in Magnus' eyes. "Whatever the question is, the answer is yes!"

"Angela, would you like to move back to Herrgott?" Magnus asked.

"Don't tease me with such words."

"I've been offered a teaching position at the University."

"Who will help Lars?"

Wilhelm apprehensively raised his hand. Angela threw her arms around the gentleman. His eyes widened with surprise. "Thank you," she whispered.

"Angela, we can set a wedding date now."

"This day keeps getting better."

"Let's go back to the farm. I have something to tell Father."

Angela's mind raced with thoughts of wedding preparations that she didn't even notice Magnus' last words.

* * *

Puffs of dust floated in the air when the courier patted his pants before entering the palace. *I look a mess, but I had to get here quickly.* Walking up the stairs, he met King Stefan and blurted out, "Sire, Anna is found. She's home and in good health."

Stefan's legs wobbled, and he took refuge in the nearest chair. "I have a letter for you, Your Majesty." The courier bowed and left to deliver his other letters.

The anticipated message had arrived at last. King Stefan's fingers trembled as he opened the letter. A smile spread across his face, and he read the letter again. Folding it up, he tucked it in his jacket. "Thank You, Lord. You have answered my prayers."

Petra listened while Ivar read his letter aloud from his twin brother, "My Dear Brother, we are praising God for the return of baby Anna and Meta. Both are well. We have many mothers and children that need help. A home for all of them is being planned. Now that our prayers are answered, Angela and I are setting our wedding date for the first Saturday of the next month. We want you to do the honor of officiating the wedding. Afterward, we are moving to Herrgott. Wilhelm will be ministering with Lars, and I have accepted a teaching position at the University of Ministry. We will be close by again! As always, your older brother, Magnus."

Ivar looked up from the letter and smiled. "My brother and Angela are getting married, and they're coming to Herrgott! He'll make a great teacher."

"Angela will make a beautiful bride," Petra added.

"And you will, too. After their ceremony, let's plan ours."

A servant walked in. "Sorry to interrupt. The king has requested your help."

Petra looked at Ivar. "See you later," she said and walked to her writing desk.

Chapter 24

Summer

Ari looked at the letter again. "It's time." Packing up his belongings, he patted his Bible. "You're coming with me this time. I'll make room." Stopping at the palace, Ari placed his Bible in the supply wagon.

Tea and Anna waved goodbye. Johann motioned his hand forward, and the attachment of guards proceeded out the gate. Little Anna wobbled back and forth, trying to follow the group.

"My last son is getting married," Ari said. "This will be a joyous day. It seems like yesterday when Magnus and Angela were married. It has already been a month."

"Papa, I wish Mama could be there."

"She will be in spirit, Son."

"How do you deal with the loss?"

"Even now, the love I have for your mother is with me." Ari sighed and shook his head. "That did not die with her, and someday I will be with her again."

"God is good, Papa."

"All the time." Ari's mind drifted, reflecting on the trials and tribulations that he and his loved ones had endured over the past year. He remembered what James wrote in the Bible, "Count all joy in trials and tribulations." *God, You were with us every step of the way, but we didn't always see it during the waiting.*

Sitting on his throne, King Stefan eyed the doorway, waiting for Ari and Johann to walk into the room. The court counselors sat in a row to his left. Ivar and Magnus sat side by side to his right.

"Magnus, give your father your chair. Ivar, give Johann your chair." The twins stood up and started to walk behind the chairs but Stefan threw up his hand. "Magnus, Ivar come forward."

The brothers locked eyes. "Did you do something wrong, Ivar," Magnus whispered. Ivar shrugged.

"Gentlemen," King Stefan began, "It is written for my son to take my throne upon my death." Stefan descended his throne and stepped off the dais. A low mummer followed. All eyes watched the king's movements.

"My son is dead; therefore, we must choose a successor, but an heir would be better." Looking at his counselors he asked, "Wouldn't you agree?" They all nodded.

Stefan picked up his book and faced the counselors. "My grandfather became heir to the throne when his older brother died. My great-grandfather loved his daughter-by-marriage and adopted her as his own." Everyone listened to the story with great curiosity. "After a period of time, his new daughter fell in love with a noble. My great-grandfather approved, but wanted them to live here in Herrgott. She and her husband thought otherwise and moved away. For a wedding present, he bought a large piece of land and built her a house and barn."

Laying the book down, Stefan motioned for his servant to bring another book forward. "This is the Bible that was given to the adopted daughter." The counselors nodded in agreement of the names recorded, the noble and his wife, the adoptive daughter of the King of Herrgott.

Looking at the ceiling, Stefan paused. "She gave birth to a boy. It was his first grandchild, and he would come to visit. Then tragedy struck. His daughter died. My great-grandfather begged the noble to come back to Herrgott with the boy."

Stefan walked over and stood in front of Ari. "The noble called them busybodies and ordered everyone off the property.

Ari, that boy is your father, Elias." Ivar's and Johann's mouths dropped. "You are heir to the throne of Herrgott."

Ari stood up. "With deep regret, I decline." He returned to his chair.

Stefan turned and targeted Ivar. "Ivar, your father has declined. You are the heir to the throne."

Ivar's eyes bulged. "But I'm not the eldest. Magnus is." Turning to his brother, he pleaded, "Tell him, Magnus."

Magnus laid his hand on Ivar's shoulder. He gave his brother a tight squeeze. "He already knows, Ivar. I have declined the offer. This is not my calling. It's yours." Magnus slightly bowed and returned to stand by his father.

Stefan lowered his head and stared at Ivar. Ivar's chest heaved in and out. The gravity of this responsibility weighed on his shoulders and his shoulders alone. His life and his future family's lives would be impacted forever. Ivar looked into Johann's eyes, looking for some type of validation of being a king.

"Ivar, looks like you'll be crowned king before I will." Magnus and Ari nodded. The counselors nodded.

Ivar closed his eyes. *Lord, what is Your will?*

A still small voice in his inner being replied, "Shepherd my sheep."

Ivar lowered himself to a knee in front of Stefan. "Yes, my king, I accept." At the same time, he thought, *What will Petra say?*

"Excellent," Stefan replied and lifted Ivar back up. Looking at the servant, Stefan commanded, "Go get Petra."

Ivar's gut quivered when Petra entered the room. Her head turned slowly as if she was counting each individual in the room. Cocking an eyebrow, she locked eyes with Ivar.

"Petra," Ivar started, "I—I have been promoted."

Petra tilted her head sideways. "What kind of promotion?"

Stefan gave a hint and pointed to the throne. Petra's jaw dropped.

Ivar's doleful eyes met hers. "I just found out that I'm related to Stefan's family. I'm the next heir." Petra remained quiet. "Petra, say something, please."

She quickly looked at Ari and Magnus. They pointed to themselves and shook their heads.

Petra mentally assessed the situation. Her life would be forever changed. She scrutinized everyone and everything in the room. If Ivar was the next in line to be king, her children would follow that path, too.

"On one condition," she finally said. Tension hung in the air while everyone waited for her terms. "That your chair is not bigger than my chair."

"Done," Stefan blurted out. "You can even pick out the colors and design."

Chapter 25

Fall

The decree had revealed many orphaned children and mothers with young children that needed help. The new king of Herrgott ordered a directive to create a home for the children and mothers. Queen Petra and her cousin, Angela, oversaw the school for the children and organized the mothers to run it. Angela taught reading and Peta taught the children about the Lord.

While praying one day, a vision of the Artz couple came to Ivar's mind. A warm glow filled his inner being, and he sent guards to the home of the caretakers of Meta and Anna.

Jakob and Hilda had just finished their morning prayers when there came a knock on their door. "Who can that be?" Jakob asked, releasing the doorlatch. A rather tall man in uniform stared at him.

"Are you Jakob?" the guard asked.

"Yes, I am."

"You and your wife are invited to the Herrgott palace as guests of King Ivar and Queen Petra. I have guards to attend to your farm in your absence and two more guards to accompany you on your trip."

Tilting his head sideways, Jakob threw Hilda a puzzled look. Hilda offered a blank face and shrugged. "We accept," she said.

Upon entering the palace courtyard, Jakob and Hilda noticed three children playing with a puppy. Ivar and Petra stood close by. Hilda curtsied to the royal couple while Jakob bowed.

D Marie

"Your children are precious," Hilda remarked.

"Thank you," replied Petra. "We bring the orphans here a small group at a time. These three lost their parents last year. This gives them a chance to play in our yard. Hilda's eyes sparkled and Jakob nodded.

The Lord heard Jakob's and Hilda's prayer. Lifting their eyes to the sky, they quietly mouthed, "Thank You, Lord." The two brothers and their sister needed a forever home and Jakob and Hilda wanted children. All five of them, including the puppy, returned to Artz.

Ivar followed them out of the palace gate and headed for the University of Ministry to share the good news. He walked past the garden that he and Magnus had tended many years ago. Entering the building, a smile spread across his face when he saw his brother in the hallway. "There's nothing like family."

* * *

Once the bridge was finished, all of the staff and craftsmen at Taulbe Castle and the ones in Christana were set free. Their skills were in high demand as they went into the construction business. A new settlement was started across the river from the castle. Their first project was a church. The detainees became the best tithers and attenders. Just like Jesus taught, in the book of Luke, the one who was forgiven the most showed the most love. The detainee with the scar on his face that Falke had put there when he struck him with a tree branch boarded that ship he had seen by the seaport in Christana and returned to his native land with valuable skills and a positive outlook on life.

* * *

Ari resumed his culinary skills. He limited it to morning meals and went to the inn for evening ones. Working with the horses didn't seem as important as it once did, but Benjamin and his brother, Klaus, loved it.

One frosty morning, Ari watched the two brothers working with the horses in the corral. Rubbing his neck, memories of the "girlfriend" episode when he teased Benjamin and Klaus during their horse training lesson produced a warm grin. But other memories drifted in, causing his shoulders to drop. "It's time," he muttered. Ari lifted his arm and motioned for the horse trainers. "Benjamin, Klaus, come into the house."

Worry covered Klaus' face. "What's going on?" he muttered to Benjamin.

"I don't know," Benjamin replied. "Let's take off the lead ropes and leave the horses in the corral."

After everyone sat down, Ari set his hands on the table and took a deep breath. "It's time for me to leave this farm. Johann has prepared a place for me with him." Benjamin and Klaus gulped, waiting for the next sentence. "The farm will continue if you want to stay."

"Yes," they said simultaneously.

"Good. My sons will not be returning. Benjamin, since you have two sons, perhaps you should take my house. Klaus, you can take the cottage."

Benjamin and Klaus looked at each other and nodded.

Ari stood up and walked behind the brothers. Putting his hands on each of them, he said, "Done. I'm packing up tomorrow."

* * *

Ari always referred to his granddaughter as Johanna. He watched her grow up and taught her how to ride horses. Little Anna had a blessed life.

One day, Ari struggled to get out of bed. "Pawpaw, let's go ride horses," Anna said.

"Maybe later, I need to rest a little longer right now."

"I'll wait for you here."

Ari smiled and rested his eyes. He woke up and saw Johanna standing by the window. He contemplated the softness of her smile and the gentle golden curls framing her face. "Johanna, I'm coming home."

His granddaughter turned her head and walked toward him. Anna responded, "You are home, Pawpaw."

"Johanna, you are the love of my life. I'm coming home."

Anna realized what he meant. *He's talking about Grandma.* Anna responded in her most grownup voice, "Ari, I love you, and I'm waiting for you to come to me."

Ari placed his hand on the locket of love and reached out his other hand. Anna held it, and he replied, "I love you, Johanna." He closed his eyes and went to the Lord and to the love of his life.

Tears blurred Anna's eyesight as she laid her head on her grandfather's chest. "I love you, Pawpaw. You are home."

Just like Paul wrote in his second letter to Timothy, Ari had won the good race and fought the good fight.

Ivar and Magnus retuned home and administered their father's funeral. The whole town showed up. Ari was known as a man of integrity, a man of God, and a good father. His sons laid their father by the love of his life, their mother, on the family farm. Ari kept his word; there was never another that could take his Johanna's place. He loved her for the rest of his life and now for all eternity. Ari's journey to be with Johanna was completed.

***

The following year, King Albert and Queen Maria decided to step down from their duties to the kingdom and enjoy being grandparents to Anna. They compiled a list of places they would like to travel and visit, especially the schools and municipal halls in each village of Christana.

"Good idea, you deserve a break and good timing for when you get back," Johann said. Albert and Maria looked at Johann then their daughter.

Tea smiled. "Mama, Papa, we're going to have another baby!"

God is my Healer

Exodus 15:26 — Jehovah Rapha, The Lord Heals

This trilogy is concluded.

God bless you on your journey.

Chapters   *Discussion Starters*

1. Discuss the importance of Maria forgiving her brother and her vision for the captives.

2. How did Gabriel's behavior, Falke's guard, differ from Lochen's, Falke's scout?

3. Arrow rock served as an indicator. What path indicators do you have in your life?

4. What prayer did Johann use? How was this prayer helpful?

5. Tea praised her parents for their example of Christian behavior. Who have been Christian models in your life?

6. The young guards at the castle were frightened and took some relief when Gabriel talked to them. Who do you look for when you are frightened? How can they help?

7. Johann experienced an odd, uncomfortable feeling. How did he get rid of it?

8. The illustration in this chapter is an actual baby bottle from the 1600s. It's ceramic. Some were made from animal horns. Contrast it to today's baby bottles.

9. Romans 8:28 is one of my favorite verses. Describe a time when this verse helped you.

10. It was not easy for Wilhelm to leave Meta, but it was necessary for her recovery. Discuss a time when you had to do something for the greater good.

11. The twins, Magnus and Ivar, are very close brothers. Who is someone your age that you are very close with? What do you appreciate the most about this person?

12. Ari searched for his granddaughter. What did you do when you lost something important and couldn't find it?

13. Think of a time when you lost someone's trust. What did you do to regain that trust back?

14. What were the two key elements of Psalms 100 that Johann and Tea discovered?

15. Why did Ari ask Ivar not to say anything about his discovery of Meta's and baby Anna's disappearance until he met with Wilhelm? What situation have you been in that required more information before you repeated what truly happened?

16. What was the desire of Daniel's heart? How did he find it? How do you share the desires of you heart?

17. Wilhelm did a good thing for Meta by taking her to the University of Medicine, but he felt terrible when he found out that Meta had left with the baby. Have you had a situation where your attempt at doing good didn't turn out like you hoped? How did you deal with it?

18. Angela was teased about knowing the names of the keys on the organ. Teasing can be in good fun or hurtful. Describe some examples of good teasing and bad teasing.

19. The Head Guard was looking right at Meta and didn't know that she was the one he was looking for. When have you seen the answer to your need but didn't recognize it?

20. What did Tea mean when she said, "I forgave you with my words, but not with my heart?" How can you be sure that forgiveness is genuine?

21. King Stefan didn't have to create a consequence for the horse thief. Why? What consequences in the Bible do we have to be aware of?

22. How was Gunther's prayer answered?

23. What did Josef put under Anna's bedding? Why did he do that? What folktale does this remind you of? Originally, I was going to write two books, one based on the *Princess and the Glass Hill* and one based on the *Princess and the Pea*. The Lord guided me to bridge the two stories. That's how the trilogy was born. He gave the plot while I wrote all three books. That is why I use a pen name and not my full name.

24. Ari's Grandmother was adopted. What rights does an adoptive child have compared to a biological child in a family? How are we adopted into God's family (Ephesians 1:5)?

25. When your journey of life is completed on Earth, how do you want to be remembered?

Reflections from the Author

Life has many choices. God wants what is good for His children. Not all of our wants and desires are good for us. We all make mistakes, and the Lord is gracious to forgive the repentant person. Holding onto unwise choices leads to self-reliance and further separation from God. We get to choose, and He allows us that freedom. Forgiveness is a priceless gift. To forgive is a healing that money cannot buy.

Lochen, the evil scout, didn't want to give up his prestige of being important and close to the power of Falke. Even though he could gain nothing from his resistance of help, he would not let go of his unwise choices. No one could change the scout's mind, only he could. He stayed in prison physically and mentally. He held the key to obtain freedom and would not use it. He would not let the Lord into his life and set him free of pride, hate, and rebellion.

Jesus has come to set the captives free (Luke 4:18). It's a promise, but the Lord will not force Himself on you. He is a gentleman. On the other hand, the enemy is like a roaring lion seeking those whom he may devour (1 Peter 5:8).

Blessed is the man who finds wisdom, the man who gains understanding (Proverbs 3:13). This passage was revealed to me when I was going through a difficult time. The Bible is like a baby in a cradle. We can't just stare at it. We need to lift the Baby up and hold it next to ourselves. Love the Word of God. Let God love you and lead you on your journey in life.

Acknowledgements

Journey in the Waiting completes the trilogy of the Journey Books of Faith and Family. Along the way, I had many individuals helping with these books to be the best possible books to inspire and support the reader in their Christian journey. I have taught school for over 30 years. Teaching a child to read is what I enjoy doing. Never in my teaching career did I ever dream of writing a book for my students to read.

I am so appreciative of the patience that my husband, Walter, had with my countless hours at the computer. It takes a tremendous amount of time to write, research, rewrite, involve beta readers, and then go through the editing process. That is one part of producing a book. Cover designs, illustrations, formatting, securing ISBNs and copyrights, making readers aware of the book… the list goes on. Through all of this, my goal is to offer wholesome and educational books for the reader to enjoy.

My beta readers gave valuable feedback. The ages range from 12 to 74. Natalia Billings, Susan Marshall, and Lynette Nelson had a keen eye and offered great advice about the characters and the plot, as well as, finding grammar errors. I am deeply blessed by their work. Susan, my sister, did overtime working with the text until it was just right.

Two teachers from a local Lutheran School read the Journey Books to their students in their classrooms. One student made the comment about the end of *Journey to the Glass Hill*. "Why did the author end it that way?" The teacher, Kathy Maske, responded, "It leads into the next book." They were ready for *Journey to the Noble Horse* to begin.

Greg Baker, Affordable Christian Editing, is the one that makes all three of my books shine. Greg, a former minister, is an author of many books, as well as, an editor. Not only did

Greg edit my books, he took the time to teach me writing skills of which I had no training. I am forever grateful for his help. He is my mentor and my friend.

Deb Jayarathne crafted the designs for all three books in the trilogy. She worked diligently to make the covers just right. After lifting those horses off of one background and placing it on another one, Deb cleaned up all the imperfections. We started as strangers and developed into friends. The white horse is symbolic of Jesus.

Brian King, a Lutheran minister, drew the illustrations for all three books. The illustrations help the reader to visualize the text being read. With a just a few simple lines, Brian was able to capture the emotions of the characters in the story. I am amazed and so appreciative of his talent and willingness to take on this extra work during his regular ministerial responsibilities.

I held a contest on social media for a chance to name a horse in this book. The winner would get their name mentioned. Roberta (Bobi) Papa was a contestant. Although her entry was considered, I liked her last name to go along with the plot. It's on page 118. The final name of the horse was entered by Cheryl Dyer. Spirit is a great name for a horse at any age. This horse was being retired from guard duty and given to a boy.

All of these people contributed to this trilogy. Without them, these books would still be in my laptop and not in your hands.

Enjoy the Journey!

About the Author

D Marie has taught school for over thirty years. She incorporated various educational methods to develop the joy of reading. D Marie designed this inspirational book as a learning tool to nurture Christian character and living. Her first two published books, *Journey to the Glass Hill,* and *Journey to the Noble Horse* are the beginning of the trilogy, Journey Books of Faith and Family. She is currently working on her next journey, tutoring beginning readers. D Marie lives in the Midwest with her husband and family.

www.DMarieBooks.com

Artists

Illustrations: Brian King is the pastor of Family Ministry at the Lutheran Church of Webster Gardens in St. Louis, Missouri. Reverend King also drew the illustrations for *Journey to the Glass Hill* and *Journey to the Noble Horse.*

Cover Design: Deborah Jayarathne. She also designed the cover for *Journey to the Glass Hill* and *Journey to the Noble Horse.*

When the storms of life rise up, what do you do?

Journey in the Waiting is the conclusion of the inspiring trilogy about two families that lived 400 years ago in northern Europe. The palace was breached. With only seconds to make a critical decision, Prince Johann sent his baby daughter away with a trusted friend, Meta. When the danger was over, he journeyed with his father, brothers, and a friend to bring them home. What could go wrong? They followed the horse's hoof tracks until the storm turned them into mud. The searchers found two things, where the woman and child had previously been and what their true level of trust was in the Lord.

The Bible is the ultimate source for Christians, but will Johann and Tea (the baby's parents) find the words there how to beseech God in their time of need? While looking for his wife, Meta, Benjamin's strong spirit waned until a young boy walked out of the woods. Ari, the baby's grandfather, stepped out of his comfort zone and relentlessly pursued the trail of clues to another country but only discovered that the missing loved ones were always beyond his grasp. Johann's brothers, Magnus and Ivar, followed a new path leading them to a destiny they could have never envisioned.

How will the Lord make something good out of this situation? What is His plan? During the waiting, will the families put their complete trust in God to provide, overcome the obstacles, and heal the broken hearted?

Made in the USA
Monee, IL
13 September 2021